Blaze

Dear Reader,

I love the Uniformly Hot miniseries, so I was thrilled when I got the chance to write another one. And since the U.S. Coast Guard is the most neglected branch of military service, I thought why not honor those brave men and women protecting our nation's borders? Immediately, I pictured my hero, Scott Everly, in action—stalwart, strong, always prepared. (And let's not forget hot and good-looking.) Everything a good protector should be.

Then came the job of choosing the right heroine for this masculine coast guard, and that's when Jackie Birchard was born. She's the daughter of a Jacques Cousteau-like oceanographer, who recently broke off from her father's influence to blaze her own trail in marine biology. When she and Scott meet, things do not go smoothly.

But love has a way of creeping up on you, and it's no different for Scott and Jackie. I hope you enjoy learning about scuba diving, the Florida Keys, marine biology and the endangered Key Bleeny as much as I enjoyed researching them. So sit back, relax and join Scott and Jackie on their Florida beach.

To see the "making of" *Born Ready,* visit my blog at http://wildelori.blogspot.com/. You'll find a mosaic collage featuring Key West, Scott, Jackie and the activities depicted in the story, along with a musical playlist of songs I listened to while writing the book.

Happy reading,

Lori Wilde

Lori Wilde

BORN READY

TORONTO NEW YORK LONDON
AMSTERDAM PARIS SYDNEY HAMBURG
STOCKHOLM ATHENS TOKYO MILAN MADRID
PRAGUE WARSAW BUDAPEST AUCKLAND

Recycling programs
for this product may
not exist in your area.

ISBN-13: 978-0-373-79662-5

BORN READY

This edition published by arrangement with Harlequin Books S.A.

For questions and comments about the quality of this book
please contact us at Customer_eCare@Harlequin.ca.

® and TM are trademarks of the publisher. Trademarks indicated with
® are registered in the United States Patent and Trademark Office, the
Canadian Trade Marks Office and in other countries.

www.Harlequin.com

Printed in U.S.A.

ABOUT THE AUTHOR

Lori Wilde is a *New York Times* bestselling author and has written more than forty books. She's been nominated for a RITA® Award and four *RT Book Reviews* Reviewers' Choice Awards. Her books have been excerpted in *Cosmopolitan, Redbook* and *Quick & Simple*. Lori teaches writing online through Ed2go. She's also an RN trained in forensics, and she volunteers at a women's shelter. Visit her website at www.loriwilde.com.

Books by Lori Wilde

To the U.S. Coast Guard.
Thank you for keeping our borders safe.

1

Semper Paratus (Always Prepared)
— *Motto of The United States Coast Guard*

SIX MONTHS CHASTE.

Coast Guard Lieutenant Commander Scott Everly had gone six long months without sex, although in all honesty it felt more like six years.

Unintended celibacy weighed heavily on his mind and body as he paddled his kayak through the mangrove channel, using vigorous physical exercise to sublimate his baser needs. He'd tried it all. Jogging, strength training, boxing, but in spite of his daily workouts, insomnia plagued him.

Digging deep, he pushed himself harder, rowing full-out until his shoulder, back and chest muscles ached with just the right kind of sweetness.

"Better than sex," he lied to himself. "Who needs sex when you've got all this?"

The early Monday-morning sun bathed warm rays, the color of Florida grapefruits, across the deep green, tree-shrouded landscape. It was good to be home again, even if it was only for three weeks. He was on leave, although the joke in the ranks was that a Coastie never went on vacation; they were born ready for action.

While he loved his commission in D.C., he missed Key West and his family something fierce. He was a Conch through and through, but when it came down to it, as long as he was near water, Scott was a happy guy.

As third generation Coast Guard, sea brine flowed through his veins, and he considered himself the luckiest man on the face of the earth to be doing a job he loved.

Scott had come home for his younger sister's wedding a week from this coming Saturday. How could it be that Megan was old enough to marry? It seemed like just yesterday that he was pulling her pigtails and putting bullfrogs down the back of her shirt.

He breathed in the heated scent of summer—ripe mangos, tangy lime, earthy loam and murky tide pools. The air smelled rich, sticky and uniquely Key West. A fish jumped, tail slapping against the water, before sinking back below the wet depths. Overhead, blue-white clouds bunched in the waning darkness, voluptuous as a plump woman's bottom. Scott had an urge to reach up and pinch the sky.

Knock it off. He was daydreaming about goosing clouds? How pathetic was that?

"Snap out of it," he growled under his breath.

It's been too long, old buddy. Way too long.

He was thirty years old, in the best shape of his life and he hadn't had sex in six months, one week, three days and twenty-one hours. Not that he was counting or anything.

His last relationship ended because his girlfriend had wanted him to leave the Coast Guard. Too dangerous, Amber had said. He'd already been injured twice. Why push his luck?

He'd flat out told her no. She'd known who and what he was when they'd started dating. If she cared about him, she wouldn't ask him to change.

She said she couldn't bear it if he ended up like this father, killed in the line of duty, and she refused to be like his mom. Widowed at forty.

Hell, she might as well have asked him to quit breathing. He'd learned one thing from that relationship. His ideal mate had to accept him just as he was—military career and all. He was done bending himself into a pretzel to please a woman.

Unless of course it was in bed.

Grinning, he stuck his oar into the water, pushed aggressively against the current. A gator slipped from the banks into the channel right behind him, but Scott didn't pay much attention. He was bent on getting sexual frustration out of his system before meeting an old friend for breakfast. Alligators were a fact of life in Florida and as long as you didn't do anything stupid, they generally minded their own business.

Six months.

The longest dry spell he'd had since college. He was a charming guy and he knew it. He'd been graced with his father's good looks and his mother's outgoing personality. Usually he had no trouble coaxing a willing lady into his bed, but as much as he wanted sex, short, hot liaisons had oddly lost their appeal.

What he couldn't figure out was why. Maybe it was because his baby sister was getting married. Megan's wedding made him realize he wasn't getting any younger, but then again neither was he ready for commitment.

So what do you want? Sex or a relationship?

That was the quandary and explained his lengthy dry spell. Scott blew out his breath and rounded the bend.

That's when he saw her.

Where the channel turned into an estuary just before it joined the sea, a lone woman bobbed in a small dinghy.

A precarious spot. Rocky shoals. Swift current. And there were the gators. Not to mention bull sharks.

Instantly, his protective instincts engaged. What was she doing out here alone at this hour of the morning when dew still dampened the air and darkness lingered in the shadow of the mangrove trees?

Was she unaware of the trouble she could get into? Between drug smugglers, human traffickers, deadly wildlife and the tourist trade that attracted scores of inebriated college students, Key West was not a place to be taken casually. As much as he loved the tropical beauty of his hometown, as a Coast Guard officer he knew all the locale's dirty little secrets.

The woman stood up in the boat, her back to him. The skiff rocked gently.

What was she up to?

She held something in her hands, but he couldn't make out what it was. Damn, he wished he had binoculars.

From what he could see of her she was thin as a sapling. Scott preferred women with a little meat on their bones. He liked rounded bellies, curvaceous butts and lush thighs. This woman could do with a double helping of his homemade chicken and dumplings. A thick slab of his famous Key lime cheesecake wouldn't do her any harm, either.

Still there was something about her that instantly attracted his attention and it went much deeper than looks. Yes, she was pretty, but in a careless way, as if she couldn't be bothered with anything as shallow as tending to her looks. She possessed both intense concentration and a quiet serenity that called to him.

She lowered whatever she held in her hands into the water via a black cable.

Scowling, Scott changed directions and paddled toward her, territorial impulses driving him. Who was she and what was she doing here?

He drew closer, but she never glanced up from her task. His kayak glided over the water, swiftly, silently. If she were up to something illegal, wouldn't she be more furtive? Or maybe she was just that arrogant.

She bent at the waist, her white cotton T-shirt riding up to expose her smooth, slender back and showing off her heart-shaped butt. From the waistband of her low-rise blue jean shorts, a red thong bikini peeked out.

Scott stared as if he'd never seen a woman in a thong, angling his head for a better look and feeling his pulse quicken. What was that all about? Normally, he was a pretty even-tempo guy and this woman was not his usual type.

And yet…and yet he could not stop staring at her.

A pair of mile-long legs tapering to skinny, but shapely calves had his breath coming out in hot, tight rasps.

Exertion. It was nothing more than exertion.

Yeah? You exercise every morning and you've never gotten short of breath like this before.

Curiosity tickled the back of his neck. Interest tingled his hands. Startling desire stirred beneath the zipper of his khaki shorts.

Leave her be. She's not your concern. You need to turn around now if you want to be on time for your breakfast meeting.

But he kept stroking straight toward her, hands curled

tightly around the bent shaft of the fiberglass paddle, because she *was* his concern. If anything happened to her, he'd feel forever guilty for not warning her about the dangers of boating alone in the Key West mangroves.

Um, you're alone.

That was different. He was a guy, for one thing, a native for another and third, he carried a gun.

Is that really why you're going over? To warn her?

Of course it was the reason. He was Coast Guard. Even though he wasn't on duty, he'd been raised to look after people on the coastal waterways. "A Coast Guard," his father had been fond of saying, "is a shepherd of the seas." The Coast Guard motto was *Semper Paratus.* Always prepared.

The glare of the rising sun caught him squarely in the face. He squinted, wished he'd worn sunglasses, his gaze fixed on the woman in the dinghy. He turned his kayak away from the sun, hungry for a second look.

She straightened in silhouette, a lithe figure in the splendid dawn. The denim shorts she wore were cut-offs with unraveling threads. One side was higher than the other as if she'd just grabbed a pair of scissors and whacked away without measuring.

Scott didn't mind. The shorter side revealed a glimpse of where her firmed thigh rounded into her buttock. He had an overwhelming urge to press his mouth to that sweet spot and nibble.

A shiver went through him and sweat popped out on his forehead. *Look away. Paddle away. Get out of here.*

He didn't move.

She reached for the hem of her T-shirt and in one quick swoop tugged it over her head, revealing a red bikini top that matched her bottoms. Although she was not overly endowed, she curved in all the right places.

More than a mouthful is a waste anyway, his best friend since grade school, entrepreneur Gibb Martin, loved to say about small-breasted women. He'd heard somewhere that the French considered the perfect breast size to be one that could fit into a wineglass. Frankly, Scott was more of a leg man. There was a reason Rod Stewart's "Hot Legs" was on his MP3 player and this woman had hot legs in spades.

Her hands went to the snap of her denim shorts and in two seconds flat, she was standing in the wavering boat wearing nothing more concealing than a thong bikini, still seemingly unaware of his presence.

Scott held his breath. He shouldn't have been so impressed. For hell's sake, women strutted the beaches of Key West in thongs every day of the week. Many of them moving straight from sand to asphalt without a cover-up for the famed Duval Street Crawl. Key West was free and easy. Residents and tourists alike came here to let it all hang out. He should not have been slack-jawed.

But he was and he had no idea why.

Sure you do. You're six months backed up and she's a nearly naked water nymph.

So he should mind his own damn business and head back. Smart. So why was he still drifting here, his gaze glued to her backside?

Don't be a tool, fool. Go.

His skin sweated against the kayak oar, his fingers curled so tightly that his short nails bit into his palms. He caressed her with his eyes from the top of her caramel-colored hair pulled back into a ponytail that just grazed the strap of her bikini top, to the nip of her waist, to the flare of her hips.

Then she gave a graceful little hop and dived headfirst

into the murky water. The muted splash echoed softly down the channel.

She disappeared from view and the last he saw of her were cute toes painted pearly peach flipping gracefully as a dolphin's fin. He waited, and his temples started to pound. He realized he was holding his breath.

Exhaling, he glanced at his sports watch. She'd been down there for over a full minute. Just when he was getting worried, she came up on the side of the boat closest to him. Talk about superior lung capacity.

Water glistened on her high cheekbones, rolled off her full lips. Her hair lay plastered against her skin. She looked like a beguiling mermaid.

Splash, Splash. Catch of the day.

Scott ran a palm across his mouth, tasted the saltiness of desire on the back of his tongue. It was too early in the morning for thoughts like this.

Her eyes were squeezed tightly shut. She tossed her head, sent water flying over him, her legs gently threading water.

Then her indigo eyes opened.

She did not startle. In fact, she seemed utterly self-possessed. As if she'd known all along that he was watching her. Who was this woman?

Their gazes locked.

A swell of thundering heat rolled through his veins, rushed straight to his groin.

She did not smile. Did not speak. She didn't have to. He could feel her disdain.

His head spun and a burst of adrenaline sent his pulse skipping. What the hell was this? Some kind of extreme horniness he'd never felt before?

He'd come over here to warn her off boating alone. Cockily portraying the protector. Donning his Coast

Guard mien. Preparing to show off his knowledge. But one look into that enigmatic face and something shifted.

Tilted.

Suddenly, Scott couldn't help feeling that he was the one in danger.

DOCTORAL STUDENT Jacqueline Birchard blinked water from her eyes. She was so wrapped up in her research project that she barely even registered the man floating in the kayak, her mind whirling with thoughts of the endangered Key blenny.

Everything was ready to go. A Kevlar cable laced with monitoring instruments lay anchored to a metal platform that extended from the floor of the estuary to just below the surface—that's what she'd just dived down to check on. She had a lab set up in the waterfront apartment she rented in town for the summer and she was receiving constant satellite feed from the underwater equipment. She had minimized all her obligations for complete immersion into this independent research project for her doctorial dissertation.

This was it. The time had come at last.

Jackie hovered on the verge of making her mark as a marine biologist and proving to her father, once and for all, that she was worthy of the name Birchard. Her success hinged on finding the elusive Key blenny.

The man with movie star good looks cleared his throat.

Jackie slid her hand over her face, dispersing the water. She had never much liked handsome men. By and large they cared too much about what people thought of them. Got too caught up in appearances. She had no patience for vanity or idle chitchat. Life was too precious to waste on the insubstantial. The planet was in trouble.

Mother Earth in pain. Global warming threatened the oceans. Mankind was rapidly working to do itself in.

She was on a mission to save the world, and with it, her relationship with her father. She had no time for pleasantries. This guy was in her way.

"Hi," he said. "I'm Scott Everly."

Annoyed at being interrupted, Jackie glowered. Ugh. It was just her bad luck to stumble across some idiotic tourist at seven o'clock in the morning. If he asked her a stupid question, she might have to hurt him. "Bully for you."

Instead of putting him off as she intended, her curt comment brought an enigmatic smile to his lips. Good God, was he trying to charm her? Seriously?

"What are you doing?" he asked, earnest as a golden retriever.

Oh, she was going to ignore that. Ignore him. This was not Oceanography 101. She had no obligation to tell him anything. She turned and swam toward her boat.

"There are bull sharks in the mangrove channels."

"Uh-huh," she said absentmindedly, her thoughts already back on the Key blenny.

"That doesn't scare you?"

Go away. "Nope."

"Why not?"

"Incidents of shark attacks are actually quite low," she said. "If you look at statistics, in Florida you're ten times more likely to be hit by lightning."

"But bull sharks are one of the most aggressive species, right behind great white and tiger sharks."

"Been watching a lot of shark week on the Discovery Channel, have you?"

He grinned. It was the kind of charismatic, come-hither grin that would have weakened the knees of most women, but not Jackie. "What if I have?"

"I'd say, don't believe everything you hear on TV."

He gave a fake gasp. "No?"

"Bull sharks are declining in number in Key West."

"Really?"

She shrugged. "People fish them for their meat, hides and oils."

"Are you a vegan?"

"No."

He cocked his head. "You're different."

Jackie rolled her eyes. Her toe found the submerged step at the back of her boat and she pulled herself up, knowing all the while he was staring at her butt.

Don't look at him. Don't encourage him.

She had an urge to readjust her swimsuit bottom but she didn't do that, either. No need to call even more attention to her ass.

But she couldn't quite resist taking a small peek over her shoulder. Not because he intrigued her. Because he didn't. Not at all. Jackie lived in her head, not her body. She was not one of those women always looking for the next guy to hook up with. Sex was fine for what it was worth, but when mixed with emotion, it invariably turned into a big hairy mess. She had no time or patience for that kind of drama.

And Mr. Perky over there looked like he was totally into the games people play.

He had a bright face, as welcoming and shiny as the morning sun. He possessed tanned skin and startlingly white teeth. His chocolate-brown hair was cut in a short, well-kept style, a poster boy for the healthy island lifestyle. He looked as wholesome as orange juice. It was enough to give a cynical woman the heebie-jeebies.

"Do you need help with anything?" he asked.

Back off, Skippee. "No."

She purposefully pulled up the white plastic milk jug she'd used as a buoy to mark this spot the previous day. It helped her find her way back, but she didn't want to advertise the location. The last thing she needed was some nosy tourist like Skippee here mucking with the expensive instruments she'd borrowed from the University of California. Which was why she was pulling up the milk jug. She would trade it out for a smaller, more inconspicuous buoy once Skippee left.

"You do realize that while the seclusion is peaceful, it's really not a good idea to go boating and swimming alone. Bad things could happen and there would be no one here to help," he said ominously.

Jackie didn't scare easily. Living twenty-six years with Dr. Jack Birchard cured her of that. But this guy was starting to creep her out. "I have a cell phone. I can call the Coast Guard."

"What if you severed an artery? They couldn't get here in time to save you."

"The bull sharks again?"

"There's human predators, as well."

Normally, whenever she was unsettled, she withdrew into her mind, where she kept a rich supply of knowledge and fantasies to ruminate over. That skill helped her survive a childhood of an absentee mother and a demanding, famous father with standards as high as the moon.

But whenever she was cornered—as she was now; she couldn't exactly go off and leave her claim vulnerable to this stranger—she went on the offensive. Another skill she'd learned from dealing with her father. If you didn't stand up to Dr. Jack at some point, he'd steamroll over you, turning you into a human pancake.

Jackie spun around in the boat, hands planted on her hips, and donned her fiercest scowl, the one that usually sent men scrambling for cover. "Are you threatening me?"

His hands shot up so fast in a gesture of surrender that he dropped his kayak paddle. "No, not at all. I didn't mean to make you feel threatened. I wasn't threatening you. I'm sorry if you felt threatened."

He looked so contrite that she almost smiled. Scott leaned over and plucked his paddle from the water, but when he raised his head, his gaze strayed to her chest. He stared long and hard. That's when she realized her nipples were beaded tight beneath her bikini top.

Men. Jackie snorted. They were so predictable.

Still, she couldn't help feeling a flush of embarrassment.

Quickly, he yanked his gaze from her chest, and met her cool stare.

A shot of pure sexual awareness buzzed into the center of Jackie's solar plexus. The sensation was so intense that she gulped to keep from taking an involuntary step backward and she brought a hand to her tingling lips.

Scott's gray eyes widened and he looked as befuddled as she felt.

Time skipped, glitched.

They exhaled simultaneously, the sound softly explosive in the balmy air. The boat wobbled. Jackie had actually been born at sea, on her father's research vessel, the *Sea Anemone,* and she always felt more balanced on water than she ever did on land. But now, she felt strangely tremulous.

Withdraw! Withdraw!

But there was nowhere to go. Scrambling to find her

equilibrium, she focused on her bare feet, pushing her toes flat against the bottom of the boat.

Scott ran his right hand through his hair. The gesture moved the cuff of his T-shirt sleeve upward, revealing a deep puckered scar on the underside of his upper arm. It looked like he'd been shot with a harpoon.

Startled, she felt a knot of attraction form in the pit of her stomach. Oh, this was crap. She couldn't like him simply because he suffered. For all she knew he was a drug dealer and that's why he'd been harpooned. Mangrove channels made for great outlaw hideouts.

But somehow she wasn't getting that vibe from him. Then again, she wasn't particularly intuitive when it came to people. Plants and animals and fish, yes. Human beings? Not so much.

So there was absolutely no reason for her to be wondering what he looked like without a shirt on. His biceps were hard as baseballs. If his arms were that awesome, chances were his abs were equally spectacular.

She did not want to go there, but her rebellious stare slipped from his arm to his chest and on down to—

Jacqueline Michele Birchard you will not look at that man's crotch.

Then something alarming occurred to her. What if he was spying on her? Oceanography was a viciously competitive field. Could he be out to steal her research project?

Don't be so mistrustful. How likely is that?

Not likely at all, but she was her father's daughter. She knew what kind of tricks people pulled to get a leg up in this cutthroat business.

Jackie snapped her gaze back to his face and said curtly, "If you'll excuse me, Mr. Everly, I have things to take care of."

"You never did tell me your name." His voice was low, teasing.

And she didn't want to tell him now. She didn't trust him any farther than she could toss him. "Jackie," she said.

"No last name?"

She hated dropping the Birchard name, but maybe if she gave him a name, he'd go away. "Birch. Jackie Birch."

Only half a lie. Still, she didn't like fudging the truth.

"Well, Jackie Birch, you have a nice morning."

"Thanks. You, too," she said automatically. All she wanted was for him to go away so she could get back to work.

"And seriously, do bring someone with you the next time you're on the water. The buddy system works best out here."

"Yes, yes." *Beat it, Skippee.*

"I'd hate for anything to happen to you." His smoky voice caressed her ears.

Then there she was again feeling completely unbalanced.

Without another word, he put his oar in the water, turned his kayak and paddled away, leaving Jackie stumped, stymied, suspicious and more than a tad sexually attracted to a total stranger.

She didn't like it. Not one bit.

2

The Coast Guard is the shepherd of the seas.
—Late Chief Warrant Officer Benjamin Everly

UNITED STATES COAST GUARD Station Key West was a
major base in the 7th District founded in 1824. Sector
Key West was a unified command consisting of two
patrol boats, eight duel boats and three small boat sta-
tions. Even though it was a small unit, Sector Key West's
responsibilities encompassed 55,000 square miles of territory, including the borders of Cuba and the Bahamas.

Every time Scott walked into his father's old head-
quarters, a thrill ran through him. This was where he'd
first fallen head over heels for the Coast Guard. His love
for his chosen career had only deepened with time. He
was living his father's legacy. You couldn't put a price
on that kind of pride.

Although now he worked out of D.C., his heart still
belonged to Sector Key West.

The place always stirred memories, but today his
thoughts stayed anchored on the woman in the red bikini.
In his mind's eye he kept seeing her standing in the boat,
vulnerable, fierce and sexy as hell. She'd said her name

was Jackie Birch but that did nothing to alleviate his curiosity.

Who was this Jackie Birch, besides a pretty woman who swam alone in the mangroves? And why did he keep wondering what she would taste like if he kissed her?

"Scott!" Marcy Dugan, the civilian public relations liaison, exclaimed. Marcy was in her mid-forties, almost as tall as Scott, with a whip-thin figure from running marathons. "It's so good to see you."

"Don't I get a hug?" He held out his arms.

"Of course." She embraced him. "It's so good to have you home."

His strongest memory of Marcy was at his father's funeral ten years ago. At the graveside, she'd placed a palm against his back and whispered, "Your father was so proud of you. I know you're going to live up to his expectations."

He'd done his best to do just that.

"How's Megan?" she asked.

"Flustered. She keeps second-guessing herself on every decision."

"All brides are nervous before the wedding. There's so much pressure."

"She really seems happy, though."

"Dave's a good guy," Marcy said, referring to Megan's fiancé.

"I'm glad to hear he gets your stamp of approval. I haven't had a chance to really get to know him yet."

Marcy smiled. "You're having a hard time letting go of your baby sister."

"Am I that transparent?"

"Yes." She linked her arm through his. "But that's okay. You've always looked after her."

"Except she doesn't need me to take care of her anymore." He was surprised to hear a wistful note in his voice.

"It's time for you to find a wife who will appreciate your protective qualities."

"Too bad you're not available," he teased.

"Flirt."

"If you ever get tired of Carl—" he winked "—you know where to find me."

"Hitting on my wife again, Everly?" Chief Warrant Officer Carl Dugan drawled as he came down the hall toward them. Carl had been born in Corpus Christi, Texas, and although he'd lived in Florida for most his life, he never lost his Lone Star accent. "You're late."

"Normally, Carl eats breakfast at 6:00 a.m. sharp," Marcy said, slipping her arm around her husband's waist and patting his flat belly. "He held off for breakfast with you, so he's bit cranky."

Carl, while good-natured, didn't believe in excuses, so Scott didn't offer him one. Besides, how would it sound if he said he was late because he'd been ogling a girl in a red bikini? "My apologies, sir."

"You can stop calling me *sir*. You outrank me now."

"That's never going to happen. I was calling you *sir* long before I ever joined the Coast Guard."

"Well, you're on vacation so I guess I can let your tardiness slide," Carl joked. "I'm hungry as a whale. How about you?"

"You know me. I can always eat."

"See you boys later." Marcy wriggled her fingers.

"You're not coming with us?" Scott raised an eyebrow.

Marcy said, "I've got a busload of middle-school students coming by for a field trip."

"Better you than me," Scott said.

"You'd be great with kids. Just wait until you have little nieces and nephews running around."

Scott put both hands over his ears. "That's my baby sister you're talking about."

Marcy laughed.

The three of them left the building together. Carl stopped to kiss Marcy's cheek before she branched off in the direction of the parking lot. "Have a good breakfast."

Without speaking, Scott and Carl fell into lockstep. Scott didn't have to ask. He knew they were having breakfast at the Lighthouse Restaurant just across the pier from the base. The familiar call of seagulls whinged overhead. The salty air carried on it a hint of coconut. Morning sun glistened glassy blue off the waves.

He paused on the pier to take a deep breath of home and Carl stopped, seeming to understand that Scott needed a moment. It was good to be back.

They walked into the restaurant, greeted by the clatter of dishes and the hum of voices. Most everyone in the place was Coast Guard of one fashion or the other—active duty, reservists, auxiliary or family members of Coasties. People waved and called out to them.

The hostess knew Carl by name and led them to his regular booth that looked out over the water.

On the wall behind them was a ten-year-old photograph of Carl with Scott's father, Ben. They wore their navy blue operational dress uniforms and had their arms slung over each other's shoulders. Looking like brothers, they grinned for the camera.

The picture had been snapped just after they'd completed a successful search-and-rescue mission for missing teens who had taken out a sailboat without permission and got caught in a squall.

It was the last photo ever taken of Scott's dad. Two weeks later, he was dead, killed in a drug interdiction operation. Psychologists might have said Scott had gone into the same line of work as his father as a way to avenge his death. They would have been half-right.

"How you been?" Carl asked.

The question was more perfunctory than fact finding. He and Carl stayed in touch through email, corresponding at least once a week. "Good, good."

"Dating?"

Scott shook his head and immediately thought of Jackie, but he had no idea why.

Six months without sex. That's why.

Their waitress came over. "The usual?" she asked Carl.

Carl nodded.

The young woman turned her eyes on Scott, smiled coyly. "And what will *you* have?"

He thought about flirting with her but he wasn't really in the mood. He couldn't stop thinking about Jackie Birch and the disdainful look she'd given him. Scott loved a challenge. He preferred to do the chasing instead of being chased.

"Scrambled eggs, four slices of bacon cooked crisp and a fruit bowl." He placed his order.

"Anything else?" She licked her lips.

"Cup of coffee."

The girl looked deflated, picked up their menus and wandered off.

"I can see why you're not dating," Carl said. "She was interested."

"I know."

Carl watched the departing waitress. "She's cute."

"Too young."

"She's over eighteen."

Scott shrugged.

"What's up? A year ago you would have been hitting banter shots like tennis balls."

"I don't know." He paused. "I guess I'm looking for something a bit more demanding."

"Picking up a young waitress is too easy?"

"Something like that."

Jackie kept prowling the back of his mind as he remembered the look on her face telling him to buzz off. He'd *wanted* to convince her that he was a man worth knowing. Why was that? The intensity of his attraction to a woman that should not have attracted him niggled.

Carl drummed his fingers on the Formica tabletop. For the most part, he was a self-possessed guy. Scott knew his friend. He had something on his mind. "What's up, Carl?"

A somber expression crossed the older man's face. He pressed his lips together, blew out a breath. "Juan De-Cristo has resurfaced."

Scott tensed, folded his hands into fists against his thighs. DeCristo was the drug lord responsible for his father's death. It had been ten years, and while the pain had ebbed, it never completely went away.

And the need for revenge? Would he ever stop feeling it?

He'd been in college when it had happened. Messing around instead of taking his academics seriously. He had wanted to enlist in the Coast Guard as soon as he graduated from high school. Ninety percent of the Coast Guard were enlisted. But his dad argued he would have more opportunity if he went to college. So he'd gone and majored in girls and good times. Then his dad had been killed and that had changed everything forever.

Scott had gotten serious about his studies. He'd changed his major to criminal justice and graduated with top honors from the University of Florida. The next day he joined the Coast Guard. They'd welcomed him like the prodigal son. He'd risen up through the ranks, working in various positions from San Diego to New Hampshire where he'd met Amber. Ironically, she'd left him just two weeks before he'd gotten the desk job in D.C.

"DeCristo is still alive?" He had to force the words through his constricted throat.

"Unfortunately. He—"

The waitress returned with their breakfast.

Carl paused, thanked her. He waited until she walked out of earshot before he resumed his story. "DeCristo was in a South American prison for a while, but his interactions there seemed to have only made him stronger. He met people. Curried favor. He's got powerful connections."

Scott picked up his fork, but he'd lost his appetite. He knew how the story went. He worked the coastal borders between California and Mexico. Understood all too well the uphill battle of preventing illegal drugs from reaching American soil.

"We've had an influx of high-grade cocaine coming into the Keys. Users aren't accustomed to such a pure product and there have been a half dozen overdose deaths."

Scott inhaled a slow hiss of breath.

"With government cutbacks, we've been in a staffing crunch. Add to that our patrol boat operational gap and we've got big trouble."

"What do you mean?"

"There's rumors that DeCristo has gotten his hands on the latest stealth technology."

That stunned Scott. This was the first he was hearing about it. Then again, D.C. was something of an ivory tower. He needed to get out on the seas more often, check on the local sonar. "But how?"

"Spies? A government mole? Hell, he could have gotten in from Russia. You're in on high-level security. You know there are leaks. Money talks and it's estimated DeCristo is worth over a billion dollars."

Scott pushed eggs around on his plate. "How substantial are these rumors?"

"Substantial enough that I'm bringing this to you."

"Details." Scott pushed his plate away, steepled his fingers, leaned in closer. "What have you heard?"

"We arrested a tourist last week who had two grams of the high-grade coke on his boat. He was looking for a plea deal and claimed to have gotten the stash from a young woman working for DeCristo."

"How credible is the guy?"

Carl shrugged. "Typical small-time drug dealer, but his story is just outlandish and detailed enough to have credibility."

"What do you mean?"

"He says that the woman told him DeCristo is using a stealth drone submarine to transport the drugs and he's using her and other young American women to help him."

"How does the operation work?"

"Supposedly, DeCristo is dropping the submarine into the water off Cuba. It's got a navigational camera that can get it through the open water, but it needs help maneuvering through obstacles in the mangrove channels. According to the source—which I admit is not terribly reliable—these young women go out in the estuaries at an appointed time, usually in the early morning or just after sunset, in skiffs with homing beacons on them and they guide the drone into shore. We haven't picked up a damn thing on our radio, but if it is a stealth submarine, we wouldn't."

If what Carl was saying was true…

Scott's gut tightened. It *was* possible. A savvy drug lord with the right connections might indeed be able to get his hands on stealth technology and make his own drone. And if he was hiring young American women to guide his drone in, no one would be the wiser. Key West was an open port just waiting to be abused.

A rushing noise built in Scott's ears, low and insistent. The hairs on his forearm lifted.

Jackie Birch.

Part of him said, no way, but another part of him, the suspicious part that had a degree in criminal justice and had worked drug interdiction on the high seas knew better. Anyone was capable of being a drug mule. From junior high school kids to grandmothers.

Jackie Birch.

It could explain why she'd been so unfriendly. Why she was in the estuary alone at dawn. Could she be a courier for DeCristo?

Disgust hardened a knot in his stomach. How could he have been so stupid? So led around by his dick?

Six months without sex, that was how.

He felt like a damned fool. *Your father's murderer is turning the Key West mangrove channels into a devil's playground and he's using gullible young women to do it.*

Except Jackie hadn't seemed the least bit gullible. She struck him as focused and very capable. A woman who knew exactly what she was doing. His stomach soured. The eggs smelled gelatinous.

"We need to seriously look into this," he told Carl.

"I was hoping you'd say that, but I don't have a budget for supposition. I have no proof beyond this small-time dealer who's looking for a plea bargain. It could all be bullshit."

"But you feel it's got a ring of truth to it?"

"Considering DeCristo's connections? Yeah, I think it's not only plausible, but possible."

"Let me do some digging."

"But you're on vacation."

"You know there's no such thing as a Coastie on vacation."

"Your sister is getting married. You've got tuxedo fittings and rehearsal dinners—"

"Next week. That's all next week."

Carl shook his head. "I told you because you have pull in Washington and I thought that maybe you could get us a bigger budget for interdiction."

"In order to do that I've got to have something stronger to go on than a rumor. I'll put my ear to the ground," he said. "You just leave this to me."

3

I will ensure that my superiors rest easy with the knowledge that I am on the helm, no matter what the conditions.

—*Surfman's Creed*

WATER.

It stirred Jackie Birchard's soul in a way nothing else did. She'd been born in March, a Pisces. Sign of the fish. Not that she believed in anything as unscientific as astrology. Her father would never have stood for it if she had exhibited a budding interest in horoscopes.

She sat cross-legged on the dumpy old sofa that came with the apartment she rented, her notebook computer nestled in her lap while she monitored the readout from her equipment submersed in the estuary. The conditions were perfect. She was determined to prove that her hunch was right.

Up until a year ago, *Starksia starcki,* aka the Key blenny, could be found in only one location in the world. Just South of Big Pine Key. But then suddenly, the Key blenny had started disappearing from that area.

Dr. Jack Birchard had been of the mind the Key

blenny was on the road to complete extinction and he attributed it to a number of cumulative environmental factors in that region. Even though he cared deeply about the ecology, her father was also the most unsentimental man on the face of the earth. Stoically, he moved on to other more salvageable creatures, leaving the Key blenny to its fate.

This was when the crack in their relationship—that had been there from the day she was born—expanded into an unbridgeable fissure. She couldn't forgive him for writing off the Key blenny.

Particularly, when he looked her in the eye and said, "It's just one species of fish. We have to focus on the bigger picture. Let it go, daughter."

And she'd made the mistake of bringing up an old emotional argument that had no place in the discussion. She raised her chin, met his challenging stare with a razor-sharp glare of her own. "Just like you did with Mother?"

He didn't fight with her. He never fought. Just issued edicts and expected them to be obeyed. If you were rebellious enough to disagree with him, he froze you out.

His eyes turned to glaciers. "You're never to mention her name again. Do you hear me?"

Okay, she shouldn't have brought up her mother. Ancient history. Water under the bridge. It wasn't as if they knew what had happened to her, although if Jackie had been truly interested, she could have called her half brother, Boone. But it had been easier to let things lie.

"You're wrong," she said, dropping the whole issue of her mother. It would always remain a sore spot between them. "About the Key blenny."

"Wrong?" He arched a skeptical brow, sent her a

glower that made her wish for an overcoat. He adjusted his glasses, narrowed his eyes.

"The fish isn't extinct."

"You have empirical data to support this assertion?"

"No, not yet—"

He dismissed her with a curt wave of his hand. "The Key blenny is a lost cause and our time is too valuable. Let's not bawl over spilled milk."

"They're not dead," she insisted. "I've tracked the current and the minute changes in temperature and I think they've simply migrated to Key West." She'd pointed to the ocean map on the wall of his research yacht. "I believe they're here."

He burst out laughing. "*Starksia starcki* has never migrated. They are not an adaptable subspecies, which is why they're virtually extinct."

Jackie gritted her teeth. Her father's arrogant belief that he knew best in matters of the sea grated on her nerves. Impossible to believe that a prestigious scientist, the oceanographer second only to Jacques Cousteau, could be so irrationally stubborn. But that was her dad. He was brilliant, yes, but his ego was the size of the sun.

"Desperate circumstances call for desperate measures and the Key blenny has risen to the challenge," she said.

He shook his head violently. "There's no coral in that area. *Starksia starcki* is a reef dweller."

"They've adapted in that regard as well and they're using the mangrove mangles for their food source."

"Doesn't happen."

"I think it *is* happening."

"Based on what?"

She explained her theory.

He made a face. "Pseudo science. I thought I taught

you better than that. You're allowing romanticism to sway your critical thinking."

She'd tried to defend her position in a calm, rational manner but he kept cutting her off. That's when Jackie knew that if she wanted to save the Key blenny, she was going to have to do it on her own. So she'd packed her things, left MIT, where her father taught, and transferred to the University of California where she was welcomed with open arms.

From a political standpoint, snagging Jack Birchard's disenfranchised daughter as a doctoral candidate was a colorful feather in the university's cap. They embraced her theory on the Key blenny, loaned her equipment for her independent study and even gave her a monthly stipend. She felt giddily liberated and wished she'd left her father's direct sphere of influence a long time ago. No more kowtowing to his diktat. She was free to explore the sea on her own. A bright future awaited her.

Now, all she had to do was prove her theory.

The hardest part was going to be keeping people away from her instruments. She hadn't fully realized that this was going to be a major issue until Scott Everly had shown up.

One minute she'd been totally isolated in the estuary, just her and nature. The next minute there had been the handsome man in the kayak. If he could appear out of nowhere, so could others.

Disgruntled, she settled the computer on the coffee table and got up to walk out onto the balcony. Sunset came quickly in the Keys and she wanted to catch it before it was gone. By dawn, she'd be back on the water. Not because she needed to go out there again so soon, but simply because she worried about Everly returning to muck with her equipment.

She entertained the idea that he might not be the simple kayaker he seemed. He could be spying on her. A competitor bent on stealing her research. Hell, her father could have sent him.

That thought was unsettling, but it was the sort of stunt her father might pull. Jack Birchard could say one thing and then do the exact opposite. The interest that the University of California had shown her project would be just the thing to make him change his mind. Except, his hubris would never allow him to admit he was wrong.

You're letting your imagination run away with you. Everly isn't after your research. He was just a good old boy out in his kayak.

Jackie leaned on the railing and took a deep breath of the sultry summer air. Duvall Street was not far away and she could hear the sound of revelers stumbling in and out of the bars that Hemingway had once frequented.

She wondered if Everly was a tourist or a Conch and then wondered why she wondered. Who cared?

The ubiquitous Key West Anthem, Jimmy Buffett's "Margaritaville," drifted up from the street. The smell of fried seafood floated along with the music. Jackie's stomach growled and she realized she'd forgotten to eat again. Her last meal had been a breakfast energy bar.

She was about to pad into the kitchen to see what she could find to eat when her computer made a soft pinging noise. It was the alert system she set up to notify her of problems with the equipment.

Quickly, she hurdled the coffee table, dropped down on the sofa and snatched up the laptop just in time to see the electronic data disappear from the screen.

A curse word escaped her lips. Either something had gone haywire with the satellite feed or someone was messing around with her equipment.

SCOTT SPENT THE REMAINDER of the day with Carl in his old stomping grounds, getting educated about what Juan DeCristo had been up to. He didn't tell Carl about Jackie. Scott knew enough about the law to make damn sure of his accusations before he threw them out there. But even so, he couldn't help wondering if there was another reason he did not mention his encounter with the woman in the red bikini.

He didn't want to admit, not even to himself, that he had been sexually attracted to her. Shame burned his gut. How could he be attracted to a woman involved in the drug trade?

Easy there. Remember, innocent until proven guilty. Trust your instincts. Your gut didn't get bad vibes from her. Don't jump to conclusions.

Still, he had to know what she'd been doing out there alone at the break of dawn.

By the end of the day, Scott knew he had to investigate and either put his mind at ease or push Jackie Birch to the top of the suspect list.

When Carl and Marcy invited him over for dinner, he begged off, asking for a rain check. He was staying in the guesthouse in his mother's backyard, but he did not even stop in to say hello to his family when he got home. He didn't bother changing out of the Coast Guard clothes he'd worn to visit Sector Key West. Instead, he walked straight to the motorboat docked at the pier and took off through the mangrove channel, headed for the estuary where he'd found Jackie that morning.

The sun hunkered low on the horizon. He'd be returning in the dark, but he had floodlights and the power of the Coast Guard behind him. The more he thought about what DeCristo was doing, the madder he got.

If Jackie Birch was involved in this, he'd take her

down so fast it would make her gorgeous little head swim, sexual attraction be damned.

Fury flamed hot inside him, burning up his collar to his neck, and on upward to flush his cheeks. He was so fired up that it took him a while to find the spot where she'd been that morning. In fact, if the dying sunlight hadn't glinted off the silver fish bobber, he might not have been able to find it in the thickening twilight.

"Gotcha," he growled and motored over.

He killed the engine and tossed the anchor overboard. Anger trembled his hand as he leaned over the side of the boat to search for what was hidden in the water. His fingers brushed a small metal platform. He grabbed hold, shook it hard.

It did not give. His fear was confirmed. Jackie Birch was up to no good.

"Son of a bitch," he swore as his gut dipped to his shoes. His stupid gut had led him astray. He'd *liked* her. Shame pushed away the anger. Six months without sex could ruin a man.

His furious fingers snatched at the buttons of his shirt. In five seconds flat he stripped off everything except his skivvies. He turned to lift up the passenger seat. He then dug in the compartment where he kept boating supplies, found a snorkel mask and underwater lamp. Too bad he didn't have a diving tank with him.

Mosquitoes buzzed around his bare skin as he strapped on the mask and leashed the lamp around his wrist. A second later, he was in the water.

Silence engulfed him. It wasn't until he was underneath the surface that he realized just how noisy it was topside—birds calling, insects singing, trees whispering in the breeze. Down here, quiet reigned.

Mangrove roots stuck out every which way, snatching at his hair, scraping against his skin. Scott flicked on the light. Fish darted past him. He examined the metal platform. It was mounted on a pole securely buried in the floor of the estuary and attached to the platform was a long black cord that stretched down as far as he could see.

He wrapped his fingers around the cord. Kevlar. He yanked. The cord did not give, but a heavy object moved, banged against the pole, vibrated the cord against his palm. Something was attached to it.

Fueled by the rumors Carl had told him about Juan DeCristo's stealth submarine drone, Scott's imagination ran wild. It could be a transmitting beacon. To elude detection, Birch could have hidden the beacon here and stopped back to attach it to her boat before each of her drug missions.

He didn't want to believe it. He wanted to give her every benefit of the doubt, mainly because he'd been dumbly smitten, but the evidence was pretty damning so far.

Don't be a chump. Let the evidence speak for itself.

He needed to dive deeper.

But first, he had to go to the surface for air.

When he reached the top he saw that heavy darkness had engulfed the sun, leaving only whisper traces of daylight lingering in the evening sky. In the distance, he heard a loud splash and tried to convince himself it was an alligator or a bull shark, and not an armed drug dealer. Precisely what was Jackie capable of?

Don't spook yourself.

He took a deep breath and dived again. With one hand on the Kevlar cord, he followed it down.

The beam of his light found the first cylindrical tube at eight feet. It was secured through the cord. He flashed the beam over the tube. It was some kind of sensor device, but what? He was not familiar enough with stealth technology to make a guess.

Air hunger drove him back to the surface. This time when he came up he saw the headlights of an approaching boat. Small craft from the sound of the engine.

Who was it? His gut roiled and he felt vulnerable, defenseless. His gun was in the boat.

The nearing craft moved at a rapid clip, coming up on him fast. There was no way he could get into his boat, get to his gun before the intruder was upon him, but he had to try.

He swam to the ladder, pulled himself up on his boat, and he was just yanking up the anchor when the headlights from the oncoming vessel caught him dead on. Now he knew how deer felt.

His soaking-wet underwear clung to his thighs. Water rolled off his body. He couldn't see against the glare, had no idea how many people were in the boat. He was an open target. He raised an arm to shield his eyes.

The engine of the other boat died.

"You there!" a tart, sharp female voice hollered. "Stop whatever you're doing. I have a gun and I won't hesitate to use it."

JACKIE WAS LYING about the gun, but she hoped the nearly naked guy poised on the back of his boat with his arm, shielding his eyes would buy her bluff. Instead of a weapon, she held a spotlight clutched tightly in her hand.

He turned directly into her spotlight, raised both arms over his head. "Don't shoot."

That's when she saw that it was Scott Everly.

The anger that had sent her running from her apartment to the boat docks and propelled her here as fast as she could drive, flared high and hot.

"You!" she spat. "I should have known. Who sent you?"

"Put away the gun," he said, his voice calm but steely.

"Who are you working for?" she demanded. "My father?"

"I'm going to put my arms down now." He started to lower his arms.

"Keep your hands up!" she barked.

Slowly, he raised his arms back up, squinted against the glare of the light. "Is that you, Jackie Birch?"

She didn't know what to do. She moistened her lips, hesitated.

It was all the time he needed. He dropped to the floor of his boat.

Startled, she moved the light to track him, but when her beam caught him again, he was back on his feet, a real gun in his hand.

Pointed straight at her.

She immediately switched off the light. It was her turn to dive to the floor of *her* boat.

"You don't have a gun, do you?" he taunted. "You're all bluster."

Crap! How was she going to get out of this? From her spot on the bottom of the boat, she eyed the keys dangling in the ignition. If she stood up, she'd be in his line of direct fire, but maybe she could ease over, start the engine and—

"It's over, Birch," he said. "Give it up."

What the hell was he talking about? Give what up? He was the one stealing *her* equipment.

Anger warred with fear. She wanted to confront him, demand to know who he was and what he was doing, but he had a gun. She had no idea what he was capable of. Gone was the affable guy she'd met that morning. In his place was a man hard-core enough to pull a gun on an unarmed woman.

You started it. You told him that you had a gun.

And she was going to end it.

She scooted on her butt until she was close enough to reach the keys, never mind the Astro Turf on the floor of the boat burning her thighs. She heard the sound of heavy footsteps but didn't dare look up. She had to get out of here before he tried to board her boat.

With one hand she started the engine. With the other, she slammed the boat into Reverse. The craft dizzily spun backward.

Jackie pulled herself up onto the seat but kept her head down.

Everly uttered a curse and a split second later the sound of his boat engine churned the night air.

Heart pounding in her throat, she goosed the accelerator and took off down the channel. She would have preferred the ocean as an escape route but she would have had to go past him in order to get there. Clearly, he would have no compunction about ramming her boat or shooting her for that matter.

Who was he and what did he want? He couldn't simply be a competing researcher. Not even her father's assistants would take things this far.

What if he was a smuggler and she'd accidentally staked a claim near his port of operation? She'd heard colorful stories about drug smugglers, had dismissed them as urban legends. Now she wished she had not been so cavalier.

Boone had told her that her single-mindedness would get her into trouble one day. She should have listened.

Wistfully, she wondered if she'd ever see her brother again. She didn't know him well, but he was the only sibling she had, the only connection to her mother.

She pushed down on the throttle, running her skiff full-out, but the bigger pursuit boat was gaining on her. The moon had started to rise, blazing a silver light over the water. Speed-generated wind blew her hair out behind her, whipping over her ears.

His engine revved, whining high and hot. In the rear-view mirror she saw him move to the left. He was going to overtake her.

Go, go, go.

But there was no more power left in her dinky boat. It had nothing left to give.

She let out a cry of alarm. What to do? What to do? She could slow down, let him pass her, try to whip around and head for the ocean, but she knew she couldn't outrun him. The scenario would be the same, only in the opposite direction.

Yet, she could not surrender. Could not give up without a fight.

You could always go into the water.

Water. The one place she always felt safe.

His boat caught up to hers. They were racing neck and neck down the channel. Mangrove trees whipped by on both sides. At this speed, in the dark, wrecking was a distinct possibility.

Dread crouched on her shoulders, but she kept going because she did not know what else to do. She'd learned a long time ago to bury her emotions. Deny them power over her actions.

He honked his horn.

She refused to look over. Fear was a marching band, ramming a cacophony of adrenaline through her veins.

Her temple throbbed. Her fisted hands tightened around the wheel. Her thoughts galloped, but no solutions materialized. She should have moved her equipment when she'd run across him this morning. Why hadn't she moved her equipment?

Because that was where her research had led her. Because in her single-mindedness she'd neglected to realize how vulnerable she was. Because she'd been so invested in showing up her father that she hadn't paid any attention to the threats around her.

Stupid, stupid girl. She could hear her father now.

Berating herself wasn't helping. She had to think. What was she going to do?

Everly's boat overtook hers. He pulled around in front of her, and started slowing down. She had no choice but to slow down, too, or ram into him.

Go ahead ram him.

Except her skiff would smash to smithereens in the process. He had one hand on the wheel, but he was looking back at her, the gun extended from his other hand. Moonlight washed over his bare chest. He was still mostly naked except for a pair of dark boxer briefs.

"Stop your boat," he ordered.

She started to jerk the wheel to the left to try to bolt.

"Don't make me shoot you," he warned.

Defeat drained every bit of energy from her body. She turned off the engine.

"Good move," he said in a tone so patronizing she wanted to smack him. He wheeled his boat around, edged it alongside hers, cut the engine.

Narrowed, steely eyes met hers. His jaw was set. His gun pointed right at her heart. "Hands up."

Slowly, she raised her arms over her head.

Time slowed, moved like syrup.

This was it. She was about to be raped or killed or both. She gritted her teeth, curled her fingernails into her palms.

No, no, I'm not going down without a fight. I'll take my last breath fighting.

"United States Coast Guard," Scott barked. "Face down on the floor. Prepare to be boarded."

4

There's no such thing as a Coast Guard on vacation.

—*Marcy Dugan, public relations liaison,*
Sector Key West

SCOTT STOOD ON THE BOW of her small craft, playing his flashlight over the prostrate woman, alarmed by the jolt of sexual awareness passing through him. He couldn't want her. He shouldn't want her.

But he did.

Gotta stop these inappropriate impulses, Everly. Six months is too long. You need to get laid. Clear your head. ASAP.

"You...you're really Coast Guard?" Relief leaked from her voice, filled the starry night air.

She lay on the floor of the boat, her hands clasped behind her back, wrists crossed together over her fanny, awaiting his handcuffs. Problem was, his cuffs were in the pants pocket of his uniform on his boat. Not to mention he was standing there in nothing but boxer briefs plastered wetly against his thighs and his half boner.

Briefly, he closed his eyes, licked his lips, struggled for control.

She raised her head from the floor, turned her face upward, squinted into the light.

Terrified that she would get a glimpse of his arousal, Scott commanded, "Face down!"

She obeyed, planting her chin back on the Astro Turf.

Scott wasn't sure what to do next. He couldn't let her up until he'd resolved his body's unwanted involuntary response. He swallowed hard.

Quick, think of something libido crushing.

But all he could think about was how long and sexy her legs looked in those cutoff blue jeans.

Scott clenched his jaw. *Global warming. The state of health care. The national debt.*

"What have I done?" she asked. "What laws have I broken?"

He didn't know what to do. Let her up? Go put on his clothes? But if he stopped to put on his clothes, she could make another run for it. Not that she could escape, but he didn't want the hassle of chasing her down again.

Scott shone the light around her boat, looking for something to restrain her with, spied a rope coiled in the corner. It was too big and thick, but it would have to do.

"The least you could do is answer me," she said. "This is pretty outrageous. You chase me down, pull a gun on me—"

"You pulled a gun on me first." He retrieved the rope.

"I didn't have a gun."

"I didn't know that." He settled his SIG Sauer P229R and the flashlight on the short bow and leaned over to tie her up.

"Are you sure you're Coast Guard?"

His fingers skimmed her soft skin as he looped the rope around her slender wrists. He could feel her breathing in angry gulps of air. The erection he thought he'd conquered stirred again.

Dammit!

Scott tugged on the ropes, making sure they were secure.

"You're rude, you know that? How am I supposed to know you're Coast Guard? You don't identify yourself. You're not in a Coast Guard cutter. You're in your underwear—"

"Lieutenant Commander Scott Everly at your service," he said. "And I'm on leave."

"So if you're on vacation do you even have the authority to manhandle me?" she seethed.

"I am when I see a crime being committed."

"What crime?" she yelled.

"Easy there, mermaid."

"Don't patronize me." She chafed.

He straightened, turned, moved away.

"Hey! Where are you going?"

"To solve the underwear situation."

"What are you talking about?"

Ignoring her, he picked up his duty weapon and flashlight and stepped back onto his boat.

"What are you doing? You're not just going to leave me tied up here!"

In spite of himself, Scott smiled. She was a feisty one. He'd grant her that. He dressed quickly, finally feeling fully in control again, holstered his duty weapon, retrieved the cylinder he'd found attached to the Kevlar cable and returned to her skiff. He reached down, hauled her to her feet and played the beam of his flashlight over her.

She sent him a blistering scowl. "I demand to know what I'm being charged with."

"Have a seat," he said mildly, indicating the captain's chair.

"No." Defiantly, she raised her chin.

He gave her his sternest military officer glare. "Do you really want to go there?"

"Bully." Petulantly, she settled onto the seat.

"You've got some mouth on you." He sank onto the small bench seat opposite her.

She narrowed her eyes, stuck out her tongue.

"Height of maturity."

"Just tell me what the hell you want."

He planed his palms over the tops of his thighs, felt the crisp material of his navy blue uniform. He held up the cylinder. "What is this?"

"If I told you, I'd have to kill you."

"Now is not the time for flippancy. You're in a lot of trouble."

"For what?"

"This for one thing." He waggled the cylinder under her nose.

"Stop it," she spat through clenched teeth. "You've messed up everything. I'm going to have to start all over."

"What is it?" he pressured.

"The ADVOcean-Hydra."

"What does it do?"

She rolled her eyes. "It uses Doppler technology to measure 3-D water velocity in a wide range of environments including surf zone, open ocean, rivers, lakes and estuaries. Know any more than you did before you asked?"

Scott studied her in the light from his boat's headlamps. Either she was telling the truth or she was a superb liar. "Just who are you, Jackie Birch?"

She pulled herself up straight. She glowered as if she wanted to deck him. He was glad he'd tied her hands. "I'm a college student."

"You seem a little old to be a college student. Slow learner?" Okay, so he was baiting her.

"PhD candidate, Skippee."

Skippee? He suppressed a smile. He had no right being intrigued by her. For all he knew she was DeCristo's drug mule. "PhD in what?"

"Marine biology. Not that it's any of your business." She wriggled against her restraints. "What am I being charged with? I have a right to know."

"I'm the one asking the questions." He pulled his cell phone from his pocket.

"Who are you calling?"

"Running a background check. Got your driver's license on you?"

She pressed her lips into a thin line. "No."

He clicked his tongue. "Tsk, tsk. You should carry ID on you at all times. Do you know your license number off the top of your head?"

She huffed out a breath. "I've got a confession."

Confession? His gut tightened. She was going to admit she was working for DeCristo. "Let me guess, you're not really a marine biologist wannabe."

"My name's not really Birch."

"Aha, now we're getting somewhere." An exquisite sadness washed over him thinking that this woman had gotten entangled with scum like DeCristo. *Don't cut her any slack. She's old enough to know what she's doing.*

"Yeah, down a freakin' rabbit hole, Alice," she snapped.

"Not really proficient in people skills, are you?"

"As if *you're* a regular Benjamin Franklin."

"Cacti have friendlier personalities than you."

"Ouch," she said sarcastically. "You are so mean. How will I ever survive a cut like that? There's a reason people give cactus a wide birth."

Scott leaned forward. This was bad. He liked her spunk. "What's your real name?"

"Jacqueline Birchard."

"What?"

She repeated her name.

An odd relief pushed out his sadness. She wasn't working for DeCristo? Why did he so want to believe that was the case?

"Any kin to Jack Birchard?" he asked hopefully.

She sighed. "He's my father."

"Seriously?"

"Yup. Happy now? You've discovered my big dark secret." Her nostrils flared.

This was the renowned oceanographer's daughter? Chagrin poked at Scott. His desire to stop DeCristo had led to a grave error in judgment.

"Wow," he said, "I'm a big admirer of your father's work."

Her sigh deepened. "Yes, yes, he hung the moon and milked the stars. Your fan worship is adorable."

"Don't get along with the old man?"

"My, you are astute. The Coast Guard must be so proud."

"It's gotta be tough living in Jack Birchard's shadow."

"You know just how to make a girl feel special. I bet women fall all over themselves to see you in your BVDs."

Scott ran a palm over his head, blew out his breath. "We got off on the wrong foot."

"Through no fault of mine."

He let the sarcasm pass. He deserved it. He'd jumped to conclusions. He wasn't normally so trigger-happy, but DeCristo's latest exploits had hot-wired his emotions. "What are you doing out here alone?"

"I was trying to find out who was messing around with my data recording instruments. Imagine my surprise to find a vacationing Coast Guard in his underwear who then chased me down and tied me up. It might be sexy if I was into bondage, but since I'm not…" She stood up, turned around. "Untie me."

Feeling foolish but not wanting her to know it, Scott tugged on the rope and it fell free, but in the process, his hand brushed lightly against her fanny and triggered another unwanted physical reaction in him. Pathetic.

He sat back, placed her monitoring device in his lap to cover what popped up.

She pivoted to face him again, brought her hands up to rub her wrists.

"So," she said, standing over him. "Who did you think I was?"

He wasn't at liberty to discuss DeCristo, but he wanted her warned. "We've had reports that drug smugglers have been using the mangrove channels to transport contraband with attractive young women as drug mules."

"You thought I was a drug mule?" She sounded amused.

"You ran from me."

"Because I thought perhaps you were a drug smuggler or pervert rapist."

"We had our wires crossed."

"To say the least."

"I regret that."

"Are you saying you're sorry?" A smug expression played over her mouth.

"No," he said, "I wouldn't have chased you if you hadn't run."

"I wouldn't have run if you hadn't pulled a gun."

"This circuitous conversation isn't getting us anywhere."

"Nope."

"I'll escort you home," he said.

"No need." She tossed her head.

"I'm not leaving you alone in the dark."

"I'll be fine."

"With your imaginary gun? What if I *had* been a drug smuggler?"

"But you weren't."

Honestly, she had to be the most stubborn woman he'd ever met. "I'm escorting you back to where you're staying," he said, brooking no more argument.

"Fine." She heaved in a deep breath and plopped down behind the wheel. "Let's just get this over with."

Scott stood. Now he was the one looming over her. "Also, I'm going to recommend that in the future you do not come out here alone."

She gripped the steering wheel. Did not meet his gaze. "Whatever."

He knew that meant that she was not going to heed his advice. "Don't take this lightly, Miss Birchard."

"Don't worry. You scared the pants off me. I won't come out here alone in the dark ever again."

It bothered him that he had frightened her, but if it had taught her a lesson, maybe it was for the best.

FRUSTRATION MIXED WITH irritation and stirred with a strong jigger of attraction.

Why did Jackie find this man sexy? She should not find him sexy. He had chased her, tied her up, accused her of being a drug mule. She should be furious. Incensed. She should have threatened to contact his superiors. She should have pulled strings. Slung around the Birchard name. He'd had no call to treat her this way. Never mind that he'd pulled up her recording equipment, tampered with her monitoring setup. And he hadn't been the least bit apologetic about it.

Would you have apologized?

No. Probably not. She had a hard time admitting when she was wrong. Her father had taught her to never apologize. That apologies put you in an inferior position.

Had she been wrong? She'd told him she had a gun when she didn't. That had been stupid, but wrong? No. She'd been trying to protect her property. Okay, maybe she could have handled the whole thing better. She could have identified herself initially. But hey, he could have been a drug smuggler.

So, in conclusion, she had not done anything wrong and she did not owe him an apology.

He probably figured the same thing.

All right. Fine. They were both right and everything had simply been a misunderstanding.

A misunderstanding that left her breathless, nipples beaded hard and a strange stirring below the waist. The kind of stirring she normally ignored.

She was ignoring it now, too. There was no point indulging a passing, inappropriate sexual desire. It would fade away. He wasn't anything special.

I beg to differ, argued her libido. *Did you see the package on him? He's got the goods.*

Pfft. And the ego to match. She had had enough of arrogant men.

Jackie glanced in her rearview mirror. He was following right behind her. Standing up at the helm of his boat. Of course he was standing up. Men with giant egos couldn't just sit. They had to make themselves as big as possible.

The wind rushed over her skin. She toyed with trying to outdistance him, but she knew he would just catch up with her and those cat-and-mouse games had already aroused dangerous feelings. She did not want to cheer on more of those feelings. Nor encourage him in any way. She just wanted to get back to her apartment, fall into bed, then get up at the crack of dawn to get back out here and put her equipment into play.

So much extra work for no damned reason. It would put her a couple of days behind in her data collecting.

She gritted her teeth. To hell with Scott Everly and his sexy smile.

He stayed right on her tail all the way to the dock. He waited while she tied up the boat. She tucked the ADVOcean-Hydra under her arm and climbed up onto the pier. He bobbed alongside the wharf. His eagle eyes turned on her. Jackie's skin warmed. God, was she blushing? She never blushed. She was thankful for the darkness. The last thing she wanted was for him to know that he'd made her blush with his hard-edged ogling.

"Here I am, safe and sound. You can leave now."

"I'm waiting right here until you get to your apartment."

"Afraid I'm going to sneak back out in the dark?"

"You're not going to do that," he said firmly.

"How do you know?"

"You're not *that* stupid. Now that you're fully aware

of the dangers in that mangrove channel you're going to be more cautious." He said it like his proclamation was a forgone conclusion. Like he knew her.

A fresh round of irritation washed over her. Turkey.

She was tempted to go out in her boat the minute he left just to prove him wrong, but she had a sneaking suspicion he was going to hang around for a while to make sure she didn't do just that.

Spinning on her heel, she stalked away up the wooden dock. It swayed beneath her stomping feet.

Behind her, he laughed low and easy.

Jackie curled her lip. She'd never met a more infuriating man in her life.

"Good night, Jackie Birchard," he called.

She raised a finger in a crude gesture.

He laughed even louder. "Mermaid, I wouldn't shoot that particular gun unless you can back up the message."

The blush that had started in her cheeks became a full-body flush as she took all kinds of innuendo from that comment.

You asked for it. You flipped him off.

Bad move. She'd keep her hands coiled tightly into fists from now on whenever she was around him.

What? You're not going to be around him ever again! I can't believe you even let that sliver of thought slip into your brain.

Well, he was hot. There wasn't any woman that could deny that. Toothy grin, chocolate-colored hair, strong chin, body like a Greek god. Seriously. He was too delicious.

Right, and since when have you ever gone for pretty boys?

There was Jed, but that was a brief descent into craziness that luckily hadn't lasted long. She'd swiftly come to her senses in regard to Jed. It had been a red-hot romance that sparked quickly and burned out just as speedily. No, if she ever even gave marriage more than a passing thought, she would hook up with a cerebral guy who could keep up with her mentally. None of those tasty morsel guys. They were good enough for a snack, but they wouldn't do for a banquet.

Her feet left the dock and hit the sand. Fully aware that Scott was still watching her, she started to run, anxious to get away from him, get back to the safety of her apartment.

What is this? Are you scared of him, Jacqueline Birchard? Since when have you been scared of any man other than your father? You don't kowtow to anyone.

She wasn't kowtowing to Scott Everly.

No? Why are you running? Why did you obey him?

He was bigger than she was. And stronger. It came down to physics. He was in command because she was a woman.

Oh, that made her madder than ever.

In reality, in the back of her mind where she did not want to admit it, she knew Scott was right. It was sketchy for a young woman to be out in the mangrove channels alone at night. All kinds of peril lurked there. She knew it, but her background seemed to buy her a lot of immunity from trouble. When people found out who her father was, they forgave her anything.

But not Scott.

He was different.

Yes, he was clearly a fan of her old man, but he hadn't allowed his admiration for her father to cause him to back down from his stance.

You like him.

She did not like him. What she felt for him was the

exact opposite of like. She loathed him. She couldn't stand him. She found him an arrogant, heavy-handed, smart aleck.

Oh, God, I do like him.

Jackie cringed, bound up the steps to her upstairs apartment. She dug in her pocket for the key, unlocked the door, pushed inside. Her heart was pounding with much more than the exertion of running the short distance across the beach.

Nonsense. This was all nonsense and she had to stop it right now. She was so close to having everything she'd worked her entire life to achieve. She would not allow him to derail her career.

No matter how much she might want to take him to bed.

It was almost 10:00 p.m. by the time Scott returned from making sure Jackie got home safely.

He pulled into the driveway at his mother's house to find her sitting on the front porch drinking a glass of iced tea laced with lime wedges.

"Hello, son," she greeted him.

"Hi, Mom."

"Want a glass of iced tea?"

He shook his head. "I'm good."

"What have you been up to?"

Scott climbed the steps, leaned down to kiss her upturned cheek, and then sank onto the lawn chair beside her.

Palm trees swayed in the night breeze. The windows were open and from inside the house he could hear the old family phonograph playing his mother's favorite record. Bobby Darin sang, "Beyond the Sea." It was a song his father used to sing to his mother. The air smelled heavily of gardenia from the bushes planted at the side of the house.

Home.

No matter how far away he strayed, Key West was always in his heart. There was no other place like it on earth.

His mother, still slender and pretty at fifty-five, wore a floral print cotton dress and a pair of beach sandals. She had her hair twisted up on her head and puka beads at her neck. "I thought you were coming by for dinner."

Chagrin pushed through him. He should have called her, but he'd gotten caught up with investigating Jackie Birchard. "I'm sorry," he apologized. "Time got away from me."

"Were you out with your friends?" she asked hopefully.

He shook his head and told her as much as he could about what was going on at Sector Key West.

"I should have known." A faint smile flickered at her lips. "You're just like your father."

Pride puffed his chest. "How's that?"

"Once a Coastie, always a Coastie."

"That's bad?"

She shrugged. "It's why you didn't marry Amber. Because she wanted you to stop being who you are."

He nodded. "For the most part."

She sighed softly. "I worry about you, son."

He reached across the space between, briefly squeezed her hand. "Mom, I'm not going to end up like Dad. For the most part, I'm a desk jockey."

"Once a Coastie, always a Coastie," she repeated.

"Meaning?"

"You can ride a desk all you want, but your heart is on the ocean."

She was dead right. He could not argue the point.

"You're going to have to find a woman as much in love with the sea as you are."

"Why do I have to find a woman at all?" he asked, thinking—for no reason at all—of Jackie Birchard. Who could love the ocean more than the daughter of a famous oceanographer, more than a woman getting her PhD in marine biology? He remembered how she'd flipped him off and he grinned.

"You don't want to spend your life alone. Trust me on this."

"Dad wouldn't want you to grieve this long," he said. "Are you dating?"

She shrugged. "Now and again. It's different when you're older. When you've had the love of your life. No one can ever live up to your father."

"Maybe they don't have to. Maybe instead of comparing men to Dad, you could see them for their own attributes."

"Listen to you. Sounding so grown-up."

"I am over thirty."

She pinched his cheek. "You're still three to me."

They sat in the dark for a long moment, not talking.

"I met Jack Birchard's daughter tonight," he said.

"*The* Jack Birchard?"

"Yep."

His mother leaned forward. "What's she like?"

"Spunky." He told her a little bit about his altercation with Jackie, leaving out the parts a guy wouldn't want his mother to know.

"She sounds like a real firecracker." Humor edged his mother's voice.

"That's an understatement."

"Is she single?"

"Most likely. She's too spiny to be in a relationship for very long."

"Is she pretty?"

"Mom, don't start with the matchmaking."

"Is she pretty?" his mother repeated.

"She's too skinny. My first thought was that she needed a big bowl of my chicken and dumplings."

"Your father used to cook for me," his mother recalled wistfully.

"Pot roast was his specialty."

"So, is she pretty?"

"Yeah." He paused. "She's pretty."

"Blonde?"

"How do you know?"

"You've got a type, son."

"Am I that easy to read?"

"For a mother, yes. Don't worry, you put on a good cryptic front for everyone else."

The conversation made him feel antsy and he wasn't sure why. "How are Megan's wedding plans stacking up?"

"You need to go for your tuxedo fitting tomorrow."

"I know, I know. I'll do it."

"Megan's boss is throwing a belated engagement party for them this weekend." Megan worked as a dolphin trainer at the Key West aquarium. "Maybe you can bring Miss Birchard."

"Mom! Seriously?"

"I'm just saying."

"Geez. I'm not dating Jackie Birchard. Even if she is blonde, she's not my type. She's too smart for me for one thing."

"Oh, she's a challenge, huh?"

"You know what I mean. She's working on a PhD."

"Sometimes it's the brainy women who really need a down-to-earth man to keep them anchored."

"You were supposed to say I'm just as smart as she is."

"You know you're smart, but books were never your strong suit. You shine at common sense."

"I made it through college."

"With a 2.8," she reminded him.

"English ate my lunch."

"But you were great at science. Remember when your father brought you that chemistry set for your tenth birthday?"

"And I blew up the doghouse. At least Rex wasn't in it at the time," he said, referring to the golden retriever he'd had while growing up.

Shannon laughed and the sound of his mother's laughter lifted his heart. "You were grounded for a month."

Scott propped his legs up on the porch railing.

"Does she like you?"

"Who?" he asked, pretending he didn't know who she was talking about.

"Jackie Birchard."

"I think the word *hate* was bandied about."

"There's a thin line between love and hate."

"No matchmaking, Mom."

"I'm sorry," she apologized. "I just want to see you as happy as Megan."

"I am happy," he replied staunchly.

"Are you?"

"Absolutely. I'm doing a job I love."

"In D.C. Far away from Key West."

"I'm here now."

"I want grandchildren. Is that so wrong?"

"Pester Megan and Dave."

"I want *lots* of grandchildren."

"I remember when I was sixteen and started dating and you told me that if I made you a grandmother before you were ready that you would—"

"Okay." She chuckled. "Point taken." She pantomimed zipping her lip. "I'm shutting up now. Your love life is your own affair, but let me just say, Jackie Birchard sounds like a keeper."

5

Once a Coastie, always a Coastie.
—*Shannon Everly, Coast Guard widow*

ON WEDNESDAY, two days after her run-in with Scott Everly, Jackie finally got her equipment working again and was back on track with her research.

Today, she sat at the bar at the Conch Café not far from her apartment. Normally, she did just fine on her own. She had a low need for social contact, but once in a while the apartment got claustrophobic, so she stashed her eight-hundred-page marine biology text and her notes and her charts in a pink tote bag decorated with sand castles and sauntered to the restaurant.

The bartender, who was an irritatingly friendly kid named Tad who was putting himself through the local junior college, let her spread her work out on the far side of the bar and didn't hassle her to buy drinks. She had a half-full piña colada in front of her, but her entire attention was focused on her work.

Her fingers cramped from all the writing she'd done. She paused to shake out her fingers, surprised to discover the ice in her drink had melted and the sun was sinking low in the sky. It had been two o'clock when she'd walked across the beach, the sand burning hot through the thin soles of her flip-flops.

She had on a simple blue tank-top dress and had her hair pulled back into a ponytail. She wore it that way ninety percent of the time. It was easier. She wasn't one for getting frequent haircuts, so that left out short hair.

"Another drink?" The bartender flashed her a cute smile.

"I'm fine."

"Anything to eat?"

Her stomach rumbled and she realized she hadn't eaten anything all day except for a handful of walnuts. "Sure. What's good here?"

"Well—" Tad leaned over the bar "—we are known for our conch fritters."

"Fine," she said. "I'll have that."

"You're pretty intense," he said. "Most girls don't have that kind of concentration. What are you studying?"

Girl. He'd called her a girl. Jackie pressed her lips together. Most women would probably be flattered.

The ceiling fan circled lazily overhead. Long rays of sunlight fell through the slats of the half-open bamboo blinds. Piped in music played "Under the Sea" from *The Little Mermaid* soundtrack. Tourist places could be so predictable, but the tune was catchy and she agreed with the sentiment of the song that it was better under the sea than up here on the surface with pesky people.

"Marine biology," she explained.

"Cool. I'm studying to be an EMT."

"Worthy career." She flipped the page of her textbook, boning up on seagrass meadows to support her theory that the Key blenny had indeed changed its feeding habits. The textbook authors weren't helpful in bolstering her suppositions.

"I was thinking about joining the Coast Guard for a while."

"Uh-huh," she mumbled, but even as she'd already mentally dismissed the bartender, his mention of the Coast Guard brought an unwanted picture into her mind. A picture of Scott Everly. The jerk.

Let it go. You don't have to waste energy on him.

"I still might," Tad continued.

She looked up, met his gaze. "Thanks for putting in the order for my conch."

"Oh, yeah." He snapped his fingers. "Right. I get it. You want to work."

"Yes. Thank you for understanding."

He flopped the white bar towel over his shoulder, looking mildly crushed and went to the kitchen to place her order.

A few single guys sat at the bar drinking beer and watching some kind of sporting event on television. Several slid her sidelong glances. She put a quietus on potential advances by sending the men a stern glower. They snapped their gazes back to the television. Good. Now where was she? Oh, yes, the sea grass meadows.

Minutes passed. Or it could have been longer. The smell of hot conch teased her nose as the bartender settled it in front of her. She frowned and pushed it off her papers, and then went back to her work.

SCOTT WALKED INTO the restaurant bar, bored out of his skull. By nature, he was not an idle guy. He had not been able to do any more investigating for Carl because of stuff he had to do for Megan's wedding.

So this afternoon, he'd had to suffer cucumber sand-

wiches, herbal tea and a collective of oohs and aahs as
Megan and Dave unwrapped toasters and place settings.
Who knew that guys were expected to attend wedding
showers? If Megan hadn't acted like she was going to
burst into tears, he wouldn't have gone. But he'd shown
up, endured and now he felt the need for a beer.

"Yo, Scott!" the bartender, Tad Winston, greeted him
with a hearty smile. "How you doin', dude?"

Tad's family lived across the street from Scott's mom
and when he was growing up, he used to follow Scott
around like a puppy.

"Never better, Tad. How's EMT school?"

"Great. Can't wait to start saving lives for real."

"Good for you."

"Beer?"

"Yup."

Tad turned to grab a frosted mug from the cooler.
"How 'bout them Marlins? Think they have a chance of
going to the play-offs?"

"We can hope, but it's only June. Lots of games between now and October." Scott settled onto the bar stool
and looked around the room.

His gaze fell on the woman at the far corner of the
bar, her nose buried in a book. In front of her sat a plate
of fried conch that looked as if she hadn't touched it and
a melted piña colada. He'd recognize that blond ponytail
anywhere.

Jackie Birchard.

There was an empty bar stool on either side of her and
he knew why. He pitied the fool who attempted to make
bar banter with her. Grinning, he got up and sauntered
over. His boring day had suddenly turned interesting.

"Mind if I have a seat?" he asked.

"Beat it, buster," she growled without even looking up.

"Friendly as always. I'm glad to see there are some things that never change."

Her head jerked up, eyes narrowed. "You." She said the word as if she were spitting out something dirty.

"Me," he confirmed, settling on the bar stool beside her.

Tad shook his head and gave Scott a you-don't-want-nothing-to-do-with-this-female-stingray look.

Scott winked at Tad.

"Buzz off," Jackie invited.

"How long have you been sitting here?" Scott asked, reaching over to pick up one of her notes.

She slapped her hand down on the paper before he could get to it. "Hands off."

"She's been here working just like that for six hours," Tad offered. "She's hard-core."

"So I see."

"What does a woman have to do to get some privacy?" She glowered. Thunderclouds looked friendlier.

"Leave the bar?"

"It's a public place. I bought a drink and food. I should be able to sit here in peace." She tossed her head defiantly and her ponytail swished seductively against her tan neck.

"You didn't eat," Scott noted.

"I've been busy."

"C'mon." He reached for her.

She pulled back, eyed him suspiciously. "I'm not going anywhere with you."

"Sure you are," he said easily.

"No, I am not."

He started picking up her papers.

"Hey, hey! What do you think you're doing? You can't do this!"

"All work and no play makes Jackie a dull girl." He nodded at the bartender. "Tad, deal with this." He pushed the plate of cold, soggy, untouched conch fritters toward him. "And place my usual order times two."

Then, tucking Jackie's books and notes under his arm, he strode toward the open-air patio.

"You…you…high-handed Neanderthal," Jackie sputtered and rushed after him.

He grinned.

"Stop smiling." She tried to snatch the book and notes from under his arm.

He clamped down, tucking his elbow against his ribs and strode ahead, making her rush to catch up. Spying an empty table in a private corner of the patio, his grin widened.

"Ape, cretin, ass."

"Uh-huh."

"You can't do this. You have no right."

He plunked her book and notes on the table. "I can and I did."

She reached for her things. He snaked out a hand and caught her wrist. She hissed in a breath as if burned. "You, Mr. Everly, are the most irritating, infuriating…"

"Keep it up, mermaid. You've got a gift for verbal foreplay."

"This is not verbal foreplay. This is moral outrage. You have taken my possessions captive. I could have you arrested."

"Not really."

"I could tell my father on you."

"Ah, Jackie, you disappoint me. I never took you for a tattletale."

That got her. She sliced him to ribbons with her prickly glare. "What do you want?"

"Park it."

"What?"

He nodded at the chair. "Sit and have a proper dinner with me."

"If that's all you wanted, why didn't you just ask? You didn't have to take my things hostage."

"I did ask."

"And I said no. No means no."

He still had hold of her wrist. He let go and she instantly brought her hand to her chest.

"What is your deal?" Her eyes clouded dark as a summer squall. "Don't you know when you're not wanted?"

"No one has ever taken care of you, have they?"

Her eyes widened and for one second he saw an expression so vulnerable it hurt his heart and he knew he'd nailed her. No one had taken care of her. He knew enough about her father to understand that man had an ocean-size ego. Jack Birchard was not the sort to pamper a little girl. He wondered about Jackie's mom, but didn't ask. There would be time enough for that when he got her to trust him.

What the hell, Everly? Why do you give a damn? You rescue people all day in your job, no need to carry it into your personal life.

Maybe not, but if anyone ever needed rescuing from her own self-imposed isolation, it was Jackie.

"You don't eat enough." He cast a glance over her thin frame. "And if what you ordered at the bar was any indication, when you do eat, you eat junk."

"So what? Now you work for the surgeon general?"

"You need to start taking better care of yourself."

"What for?"

"So you'll have the energy for all the important work

you're doing." He nodded at the book and notes sitting in the middle of the wrought-iron table.

That softened her. She cared about her research. Maybe it was the only thing she did care about. That and impressing her father. Yes, he could figure that out about her, too. If you had a father like Birchard you'd have to constantly prove yourself.

"Sit down," he said more gently and took the other chair parked at the table.

Slowly, anger draining from her face, she eased onto the edge of the chair and perched like a hummingbird at red honeysuckle bloom, prepared to zip away at the first sign of danger.

"Okay, here I am sitting down. Now what?"

"We have a nice meal."

"That's it?"

"That's it. All you have to do is eat something healthy."

"I don't have to talk to you?"

"Silence works for me."

She stared at him.

Scott smiled.

Jackie fought the smile tipping at her own lips, and settled her hands in her lap.

The sound of the ocean lapping against the shore reached their ears along with the soft tones on the sound system playing "Edge of the Ocean" by Ivy.

"I'm not talking. Just eating."

"Fine."

"You can't make me have a conversation with you."

"Jackie," he murmured. "I can't make you do anything."

"Darn Skippee."

He stacked his hands on the table.

She held his eyes with one of the most penetrating stares he'd ever encountered. She was brave. He liked that about her.

"Here you go," Tad said.

Simultaneously, Scott and Jackie glanced up as the smell of broiled seafood curled around them. Scott moved Jackie's books to one side of the table and Tad settled their plates in front of them.

"Thank you, Tad," Scott said.

Jackie picked up her fork.

"Tell Tad thank-you," Scott prodded.

She looked chagrined. "Thank you, Tad."

"You're welcome." Tad grinned.

Once Tad was out of earshot, Scott leaned back in his seat and studied her a long moment.

"What?"

"You're cunning and brave, but you have zero social skills. I'm beginning to think you were raised by wolves."

Startled eyebrows bounced up on Jackie's forehead. "You think you're really insightful, don't you?"

He shrugged. "Eat."

"I'm not talking."

"So you said." He unfurled the paper napkin wrapped around his silverware and spread it over his lap.

"This does smell good," she admitted.

"And it's a lot healthier than fried conch."

"I thought everyone on Key West adored fried conch."

"I didn't say it wasn't good. It's just not good for you."

Jackie stabbed a rum-glazed broiled shrimp with her fork, slipped it into her mouth. "Oh, this is good."

"Wow, you said something positive and complimentary."

"Don't be sarcastic. It doesn't suit you."

"Leave the sarcasm to you, huh?" He speared a hunk of bib lettuce dressed with lime vinaigrette.

"Something like that."

They ate in silence for a few minutes.

"How's the Coast Guard business?" she asked after a while.

"Excuse me? Are you actually making polite conversation?"

"I'm trying here. Cut me some slack."

He raised his palms. "Consider the slack cut."

"How come a hunky guy like you isn't married?"

"You think I'm hunky." He couldn't help smirking.

"Don't gloat. I don't want to upchuck this beautiful shrimp."

"Good food, isn't it?"

"Great," she admitted. "I had no idea I was so hungry."

"I'm glad you're enjoying it."

"You never answered my question. Why hasn't someone snatched up an eligible bachelor like you? You're like, what? Thirty-five?"

"Thirty-one," he said around his bruised ego.

"Or have you already been married and divorced?"

"No one's ever slipped a ring on this finger." He held up his bare left hand.

"So what? You got terminal bad breath or something?"

"Just haven't found the right woman I guess."

"What about her?" Jackie waved a hand at a waitress delivering food at the next table over.

"No thanks."

"How come?"

"Too young." He held her gaze.

She didn't flinch. "She looks over eighteen to me. What's wrong with young?"

"I'd have to teach her everything. I'd rather have someone who knows her way around the world."

"Never know. She might be able to teach you a few things about taking orders."

"Maybe you should date her," Scott joked.

"Are you saying I don't take direction well?"

"I'm saying you'd wash out of the Coast Guard on the first day."

"Good thing I have zero interest in joining the Coast Guard."

Scott chuckled.

"I don't get it," she muttered.

"Get what?"

"Why you seem to like me."

"Abrasive, obsessive, cranky, what's not to like?"

"If I'm so bad, why are you here?"

"I'm one of those guys who believes you can't enjoy the sunshine without a little rain. How can I enjoy a pleasant woman without spending a little time with a shrew?"

"I'm not a shrew. I just have different priorities than most women."

"I know." He sobered. "I was just teasing. I don't think you're a shrew."

"I can be," she admitted. "When my research gets stymied."

"And I stymied it when I pulled up your equipment."

"Yes." She lowered her eyes, gazed at him speculatively. "But all is well now. I forgive you."

"Thanks," he said, feeling strangely, incredibly relieved. The tone of the evening changed after that and they chattered leisurely about their mutual love of the ocean for almost an hour. Every time he peered into her eyes, Scott felt swept away. *Everly, something weird is going on here. Just pay the bill and leave while the getting is good. She won't take offense.*

Yes, right, good idea. That's exactly what he would do. He pulled his wallet from his pocket, peeled off the money for the meal, plus a sizable tip for Tad, and tucked the cash under his empty plate.

He stood up, leaned down.

Jackie sat in the chair looking up at him. He admired her at close range. Moonlight draped over her patrician features. Her skin shimmered golden. The ocean whispered.

Mermaid.

He opened his mouth, meant to tell her good-night, good luck with her studies, have a good life, but instead, he said, "C'mon. I'll walk you home."

JACKIE DID NOT WANT to admit that she was enjoying herself and Scott's company. She wasn't prone to infatuation. If she felt lusty, she usually took care of it in the most efficient way possible, got the urges out of her system and then went back to work. She found anything that distracted her from her research an irritant.

But now, here, walking along the beach with her sandals clutched between her fingers, her feet digging into the sand, the sound of the surf whispering a sweet lullaby, and Scott walking beside her, she felt…well…feminine.

Normal.

Startled by this thought, she drew in a deep breath. Who was this guy and why was he interested in her? Bigger question, why was she interested in him? Yes, she was interested. There. She'd dared to admit it.

He carried her book and notes under his arm. She sneaked a glance over at him. The moonlight cast his profile in shadows. He had a strong nose and an equally strong chin, high cheekbones and piercing eyes. Her stomach jumped at the acknowledgment of her desire.

Hormones. Chemicals. That was all.

She was a scientist. She understood that. It was okay. Part of the human condition. One thing she did not believe in was the softer feelings of the heart. Emotions were transient. Shifting. As evidenced by her parents' tumultuous relationships and her mother's abandonment. She pushed that thought aside. She didn't even miss her mother. Not really. Not anymore. She'd learned to comfort herself with science. Jack had taught her that. Her father had his faults, but he'd stuck by her and he'd shown her that the best way to cope with emotions was simply to ignore them.

Weigh the facts, evaluate the empirical data, draw rational conclusions from the evidence, don't allow your mind to be swayed by anything as ethereal as emotions.

So perhaps that was why she was so startled by the strength of attraction she felt for Scott Everly.

Let it go. It will pass.

She took a deep breath, watched the moonlight shimmer over the water.

The ocean.

The one thing she truly loved unequivocally. As unfathomable as the ocean was, she understood it far more than she understood human nature.

Scott, on the other hand, seemed to have a knack for reading people. It was a knack she envied. A knack that made her feel ineffective and socially backward.

"I love the ocean," Scott murmured.

"What's not to love? It's mysterious and haunting. Thrilling and calming all at the same time."

"Yeah." His voice husky.

She could feel the heat of his gaze upon her. She stopped, turned away from him and toward the sea. "I suppose it's the one thing we have in common."

"You don't know me well enough to say that." He moved to stand beside her. He was so close all she had to do was reach out and touch him.

Do not touch him.

"Do you like scuba diving?" he asked.

"I took my first dive when I was seven," she said.

"I was six."

"Show-off."

"When your father is Coast Guard, you learn early."

"Or when your dad is Jack Birchard."

"That's got to be weird."

She shrugged. "To me, it's normal."

"There is nothing normal about you, mermaid."

She knew that. A pang of something she could not name squeezed her. "Why do you call me that?"

"It's the first thought that popped into my head when I saw you on your boat. Now here's a mermaid."

"What made you think that?"

He didn't answer for a while. She could hear the sound of his breathing.

"When I was a kid I had a crush on the Little Mermaid. Not the Disney version, but the Hans Christian Andersen story. My father read it to me as a bedtime story."

Jackie imagined a young Scott curled up in a bed with seascape sheets and models of Coast Guard helicopters and cutters dangling from the ceiling. The strange twist in her stomach tightened. "Guess what my father read me as a bedtime story."

"Oceanography text books."

"That and his biography."

"Jackie," he whispered, sympathy oozing in his tone.

She laughed off his compassion. "It's okay. He is the greatest oceanographer in the world next to Jacques Cousteau. What do you suppose the deal is with the name Jack? Name your kid Jack and he's bound to go to sea?"

"Or name your daughter Jackie?"

"That was just an ego thing for the old man."

"Excuse me for saying so, but he sounds like a total prick."

Defensively, she shrugged. "He's not. Not really. He's just too busy saving the world to bother with human niceties."

"And it rubbed off on you."

It had. Guilt nibbled at her. She had been pretty rude to Scott from the very beginning and yet, here he was, still trying to break through the barnacles she'd built around herself to stay safe. Part of her appreciated his efforts, but on another level, he totally terrified her.

"It's getting late," he commented.

"Yes." She turned and started walking.

Scott stayed right beside her, step for step.

They reached her apartment. She stopped at the bottom of the stairs. "This is me. Good night."

"I'm walking you all the way to your front door."

"There's no need."

"I didn't ask if there was a need. I said I was walking you home and I'm walking you to your door."

She turned away so he couldn't see her smile and she started up the steps. He came up behind her, his feet echoing heavily on the metal steps. She fished her keys from her pocket at the door.

He clicked his tongue in that tsk-tsk way he had. "You didn't leave your porch light on."

"I never do."

"Why not?"

"I forget."

He shook his head. "I shudder to think of all the other safety measures you skimp on because your head is in the clouds."

"Are you calling me an airhead?"

"Not at all." Humor tinged his voice. "You're a bona fide seahead."

She laughed. "Well, thank you for walk—"

Jackie didn't get the rest of the sentence out. She heard her book fall from his arm. It hit the landing with a loud plop and papers flew up everywhere. She should have been alarmed by that. Should have scrambled to retrieve her data.

Instead, when Scott wrapped an arm around her waist and pulled her up tight to his chest, she sank against him.

No, no, this is not smart. Not smart at all.

But she stilled the intelligent voice warning her to stop this nonsense right now. And when his mouth covered hers, she actually sighed, breathing in the taste of him.

His impish tongue skimmed her lips and damn if she didn't part her teeth and let him slip right in.

"Jackie," he whispered against her mouth.

The sweet vibration sent a shiver through her. How long had it been since a man had kissed her? Over a year. Maybe much longer.

He kept kissing her. Lightly. With much care. The gentle brush of angelfish.

The kiss deepened, sweetened.

Scott. Scott. His name took front seat in her mind. She'd been schooled to reject anything unscientific, anything that smacked of romance, but in that moment, Jackie felt her beliefs shift and another word settled in beside Scott's name.

Magic.

His arm tightened around her and she pressed her palm against his chest. Felt the pounding of his heart. His pulse bounding quick as hers.

They searched for, and found, a more intimate fit. Their mouths blooming in urgent commingling. A rush of blood. A thrust of hearts.

Then Scott broke the kiss, stepped back.

Disoriented, slightly dizzy, Jackie sank back against the door, realized her legs were scarcely able to bear her weight.

"I think it's time I headed home."

"Yes." She cleared her throat. *Don't go.* "Yes."

He didn't move.

Neither did she.

"I know you're busy," he said. "But everyone needs to take a break and, honest to Pete, Jackie, I'm bored out of my skull on vacation. I was wondering…"

She met his gaze. "Are you asking me out?"

"Scuba diving. Dry Tortugas. You up for it?"

She should say no. She was already behind on her work. Usually, she would say no. There was no real reason to say yes. None at all.

Except she wanted to go.

She shook her head. "Really, I can't."

He looked sheepish. "No problem. I figured it was worth a shot." He picked up her book and papers, passsed them to her, then turned to go.

Jackie unlocked her door. Heard his footsteps on the stairs. "Wait."

He stopped, turned back.

"I do love the Dry Tortugas."

The spontaneous grin that took his face hostage, tugged at her. "No kidding."

"I'd love to go with you," she said, knowing it was probably a stupid thing to say.

"Great." His gaze held her. "Pick up you tomorrow at dawn."

With that, he was gone, taking the steps two at a time, and as he disappeared down the beach, Jackie heard him whistling "Beyond the Sea."

6

When you're being swept overboard, it's a good
idea to have a Coast Guard at the helm.
—*Jacqueline Birchard, marine biologist*

DURING HER TWENTY-SIX years on earth, Jackie had dived
countless times, but each time she went under the surface, it was different. And each time she went down into
the deep blue, her heart filled with joy. This time, with
Scott, there was an entire new element. An aspect she
had not expected, nor prepared for.

For one thing, he was as comfortable on the water as
she was. During the two-and-a-half-hour trip to the Dry
Tortugas in his speedboat, they hadn't spoken a word,
both of them enjoying the sun and the bounce of the boat
on the waves. She felt like a schoolgirl playing hooky,
except she'd never played hooky in her life.

The Dry Tortugas were a group of small islands, com-
posed of sand and coral reef, seventy miles south of Key
West. They were known for their thriving marine life
and old Fort Jefferson, which was started in the mid-
nineteenth century and never completed. The islands
were rife with romantic tales of pirates, sunken ships

and hidden treasures. There was a natural research area in the Tortugas and it was a place her father visited often.

When they reached the diving spot, neither of them spoke. They just started working like a team, as if they'd been doing it for years. Jackie dropped anchor, while Scott set their diving tanks upright on the boat.

With practiced movements, they checked the O-ring channel on their tank valves and then moved on to get their vest straps wet, leaning over starboard at the same moment. Once they'd wetted them, they loosened the straps on their buoyancy control devices, called BCDs for short, slipped them over the air tanks and lowered them until the BCD was fully snug and locked with the tank strap.

They attached the regulators, then positioned and tightened the yokes over the tank valves. They purged the valves, listening for the sound of air. They checked the gauges and made sure there were no leaks. Precision counted in diving. Skip a step, allow diligence to slip and you could die down there. When they realized they were in perfect synchronicity, their eyes met and they smiled at each other.

Quickly, feeling oddly embarrassed, Jackie glanced away. If she hadn't been so excited about diving, she might have run away. Instead, she sat on the edge of the boat and just dropped backward into the ocean, letting the waves envelop her in a welcoming hug.

Scott followed right behind her.

In tandem, they swam toward the coral reef.

Her heart beat faster as she breathed in from her tank. The familiar gurgle of bubbles was music to her ears.

Yes. Home. She was home.

Maybe she was something of a mermaid at that. Was

it odd to feel more joyous in the water than she ever did on land?

Underneath the surface there lay a beautiful garden nondivers never saw for themselves. Stony coral formed the basis of the living architecture. The reefs were a unique ecosystem made up primarily of calcium deposited by marine life such as jellies and anemones.

Jackie's gaze was immediately drawn to the exquisite coral sculptures and the other creatures that made their homes in the reef. There was always so much going on here. Gorgeous green *Zooxanthellae*. The spotted *Plectorhinchus chaetodonoides,* also known as Harlequin sweetlips. The vibrant purple-and-yellow fairy basslets. The aptly named jewelfish, who shimmered with golden sparkles. It took her breath every single time.

Scott tapped her shoulder, pointed out the moray eel swimming by. She couldn't see his smile, but behind his protective goggles, his eyes shone as excited as she was.

This man was different.

Stop thinking like that. It's counterproductive.

Why?

Um, well because...

Can't think of any reason, can you? Just enjoy the ride for once, Jackie.

And so she did, swimming alongside as they explored the reef, spotting rainbow parrot fish, elegant stingrays, vibrant red sea stars, and schools of glassy sweepers that moved in perfect unison, prettier than clouds.

Florida was one of the most fascinating places on earth. In Jackie's mind the only other locale that could rival it for sheer divine pleasure was the Great Barrier Reef.

She would love to dive the barrier reef with Scott.

Well, you're not going to. Seriously. Stop thinking like this.

Yes, right. She was getting back on track. A Goliath grouper swam by. She hadn't seen one of them in years. She reached to poke Scott's ribs to point it out. The contact with his muscled rib cage underneath the spongy, smooth material of his wet suit created a rippling sensation in her belly. She gulped and felt as if she was treading water for her life. Floundering.

Scott's face was in front of her. And she calmed. Why? How did he cause both a serene peace and a raging fire inside her? She sucked in air.

His eyes crinkled and she knew he was grinning.

Did he feel it, too? Or was she imagining all this?

She longed to swim away, but knew she couldn't. Instead, she followed his lead. They darted like spadefish and she felt as sexually charged as a dolphin. Most people didn't realize precisely how horny those adorable creatures really were.

You are not a dolphin. Stop thinking dolphin thoughts.

But right now she wished she *was* a dolphin. If she was a dolphin, she and Scott would be mating like crazy right now and not caring what it meant.

Jackie's face heated.

Scott turned and his leg brushed against hers, stealing all the breath from her lungs.

Breathe. Just breathe.

What if you made love to him? Followed your female instincts? As long as you took precautions, there wouldn't be anything wrong with it.

Having sex with him would release a lot of tension. She could calm down, relax, fully concentrate on her work. This outing was great recreation for her mind. Why not allow her body the same pleasure?

Yes, yes. I like this idea, whispered her impish id. *Do it, do it.*

You would, you naughty wench, chided her judgmental superego.

Turn off the running commentary, Jackie. You're missing the moment.

The environment around her was mesmerizing. Incredible. The colors. The movement. From the plethora of clownfish to the fluttering of purple sea fans.

Scott rolled over on his back, kicked his fins. He looked so sexy. A lump blocked her throat. She wanted him. Wanted to lick her tongue over that hard body. Wanted to feel him buried inside of her. It had been so long since she'd felt this much sexual desire.

Honestly, had she ever felt this much sexual desire?

It raged against her pelvis. Need. Longing. Wide as an ocean.

Why not? Why not?

She inhaled, pulled oxygen deeply into her lungs, felt as if she were drowning. But how could she drown? She was a mermaid after all. Born and raised in the water.

Scott pointed at his watch, and then motioned toward the surface. She glanced at her own watch, was startled to see they'd been down almost an hour. How was that possible? It seemed just a few minutes. She nodded.

He kicked toward the surface.

Jackie rolled on her back and watched him go, imagined herself settling to the bottom of the ocean, letting it claim her.

Why did she feel so conflicted? On the one hand, she wanted him with a fierceness that scared her. While at the same, she wanted to swim as far away from him as she could get.

She'd never been so mixed-up. Determination had

controlled her life for as long as she could remember. She knew she was single-minded. Some might say self-absorbed. But it wasn't her own consciousness that interested her. Rather it was the mysteriousness of the sea.

You might be under the water, but you're still in an ivory tower. You might have distracted yourself from the outside world with marine life, but you're still trapped inside your own head.

It was true and suddenly, she experienced a bone-deep loneliness pressing down on her. The loneliness had been there for years but she'd learned how to ignore it. How to muscle it aside with her obsession.

Oh, dammit. What was going on here?

Scott Everly.

He was the cause of her disturbance.

You can't stay here. He won't let you be. You know he'll come after you.

First time. First time ever that a man had pursued her this relentlessly. She'd tried her best to shove him away, but he refused to be pushed.

She watched him break the surface, knew she had to go. She shook off the languor that possessed her and followed him toward the sun.

TEN MINUTES LATER, after they'd shed their diving tanks and put away their equipment, Scott straightened, pushed a hand through his hair and gifted her with a heart-stopping smile.

Fierce.

She wanted him something fierce. The kiss he'd given her last night had been kind and gentle and tender. But Jackie had grown up on a fierce sea with a fierce father and the fierce loss of her mother. She was fierce. It was in her DNA.

Need pushed her. Desire muddled her brain. Lust flung her headlong toward him. She covered the distance between them in three running strides and launched herself into his arms.

Wide-eyed with surprise, Scott's mouth rounded into a wide O. Jackie planted a kiss on him, with as much finesse as a doberman. Default mode. Take no prisoners.

His limbs stiffened.

What was wrong?

Wrong? *How do you expect him to react?*

Like a guy. Take her right now here on the bottom of the boat. Just as she hoped. Yeah. That's what she wanted.

Stupid. You don't have a condom. Why did you start this? You're coming across as a sex-crazed lunatic—

And then his mouth came to life beneath hers. His tongue darting between her teeth like blushing wrasse—quick and stealthy. Stealing precious air from her lungs in hungry sucking gulps.

Okay, so it wasn't the smoothest kiss ever, but man, was it potent. Full of lusty energy and the flavor of the sea. Salty. Fierce. Just what she needed. *Yeah, baby. Take me down.*

Scott pulled her off her feet, pressed her hard against his body. He was aroused. No doubt about it. His erection poked insistently beneath his swim trunks. She tightened her arms around his neck, slackened her jaw. Gave him full access.

He kissed her hot and hard. Just like she wanted it. No hint of romance. All pure, hot sex.

Yes, yes.

His tongue was a thing of wonder. She had no idea that tongues even knew tricks like that. Stroking, gliding, tickling. She moved her pelvis against his, knocking him off balance. He tumbled back, but never let go, breaking her fall as they landed on the bottom of the boat with Jackie straddling him.

"Hurricane Jackie," he croaked.

She leaned down to kiss him again, heedless of everything except her desire.

"Whoa, hold on." He turned his head and her lips landed on his cheeks.

"What?" she gasped.

"Much as I want you, mermaid, this is neither the time nor the place."

"Why not?"

"For one thing, anyone could motor by at a moment's notice."

"So?" she said. "That's what makes it so exciting."

He raised a palm. "I'm not a wham-bam-thank-you-ma'am kind of guy."

"You can change your M.O. this once."

"Sorry. I'm like a manatee. Slow and careful. For another thing, we have no protection."

She groaned. He had her there.

"You don't fool around. When you want something, you go for it."

"Yeah, well." She rolled off him, lay splayed on her back staring up at the white clouds puffing and swelling in the sky. "I'm coming to my senses. Thanks for putting the brakes on. The last thing we need is to have sex."

"No, no." He sounded alarmed. "That wasn't the direction I meant for this to go."

"Look, when you're hanging out with me, you take it where you can get it, when you can get it."

Scott's expression ironed flat. "Am I with you, Jackie?"

She blew out her breath. "You're here now. Let that be enough."

He said nothing, but his eyes darkened.

Unsettled, her stomach listed. "What?"

"I think we could find a compromise in there somewhere, don't you."

"Nope." She hopped to her feet, experiencing so many emotions at once that she felt claustrophobic. "You had your chance and you blew it."

"You're not serious." Scott sat up.

She shrugged. "I am."

"Hmm."

"Hmm, what?"

"We'll have to see about that. No one runs this hot and cold."

"I'm not a woman who normally follows my impulses, so when I have them and I do follow them, it's a one-shot deal. Now that I've had time to think this through I see what a really dumb idea this was."

"Jackie," he coaxed.

She blew out her breath. "What?"

"You're playing games."

She shook her head. "I'm not a game player."

"Maybe not normally, but you are right now." He pulled himself up on the bench seat. She couldn't help noticing that he was still as hard as a steel rod.

"We can discuss this like rational adults." He patted the seat beside him. "No freaking out required."

"Fine." She sat beside him. Crossed her legs. Forced herself not to look at his boner. "What do you want to talk about?"

"You. Me. This."

"Do we really have to talk?"

"I want you. Clearly you can see that."

"Um, yeah."

"And from that kiss, I surmise that you want me, as well."

"Wanted. I wanted you. It passed. I'm over it."

"Your nipples are still as hard as pebbles. I can see them through your bikini top."

She crossed her arms over her chest. "Stop looking."

"There's nothing wrong with having sexual desires."

"I never said there was."

"What are you so afraid of?"

"Complications. I don't do complications. I'm a single-minded grad student."

"It doesn't have to be complicated."

She raised an eyebrow. "No?"

"You're surprised?"

"You just seem like the kind of guy who needs to take care of a woman. I don't want to be taken care of. Other than in a sexual way."

"Jackie Birchard." He held out his hand. "I'd love to dive down to the bottom of the sexual sea with you."

"That's it? Nothing more?"

"Nothing more."

"You won't try to take care of me?"

"Promise." He kept his hand extended. "Hot sex. No strings attached, if that's what you want. Agreed?"

"No strings attached," she echoed, sank her hands into his, feeling as if she'd gotten a great deal for a rock-bottom price.

WHAT HAD HE AGREED TO?

As Scott drove the boat to the Dry Tortugas, where he'd planned to spread out the picnic lunch he'd prepared for their outing, he couldn't help feeling like he'd stepped off a high-diving board and was tumbling to the bottom of an endless sea. What was it about Jackie that pulled him down into a headlong descent?

From his position behind the wheel, he sneaked a glance over at her.

She sat on the bench seat beside him, her head thrown back, her eyes closed, gorgeous face upturned to catch the wind. Her long damp hair whipped wildly in the air. A faint smile tipped the corners of her mouth. She looked completely happy.

Mermaid.

His ravenous gaze traveled from her face down the column of her long, slender neck to the hollow of her throat. He could see her pulse beating strong and steady. He moistened his lips. His tongue still tingled from the heady taste of her. Salt and sea. It was his favorite flavor. He'd finally found a woman who loved the sea as much as he did. Maybe more. And he'd just vowed to keep their relationship strictly sexual.

So what's the problem?

His gaze tracked lower, took in the gentle swell of her breasts beneath the functional black bikini. It wasn't a particularly sexy swimsuit, but in Scott's eyes she couldn't have looked more like a pinup queen. Sweat popped out on his forehead and it wasn't from the heat. The day was pleasant. Warm, but not hot. He brushed the back of his hand over his brow.

Jackie shifted, her lithe body moving.

Oh, hell. What had he gotten himself into?

Her flat, taut belly had him wanting to spread the picnic over her skin and nibble it off.

Pervert.

Yes. He was. His mind filled with images of all the things they could do with the food in the picnic basket.

He imagined pouring champagne into the delicious scoop of a navel and then dipping fresh strawberries into it.

Bam!

His boner was back with a vengeance.

He thought about the way she'd come at him earlier. Kissing him with such passion that she'd knocked him on his ass. The woman was a hurricane. She might be smart and keep herself isolated behind a wall of books and knowledge, but she had a wild streak that he was just itching to explore.

"Are you still making love to me with your eyes?" she asked lazily, her own eyes closed.

"How…" His voice cracked. "D-did you know?"

"Please. You're a man. I'm a half-naked woman. You do the math."

"You're not timid about sex."

She arched her back. "What's to be timid about? Sex is sex. As long as you don't mistake it for something else, there's nothing to be scared of."

Yeah, see, that was the thing. Scott could visualize this being about far more than just sex. At least for him.

Then for hell's sakes, Everly, don't make love to her.

But six months celibate, he was hurting so badly that he could barely think.

Jackie opened one eye and studied him. "You look pale."

"Me?" He bluffed. "I'm fine."

"You sure?" A sly smile crinkled her eyes.

She was so enticing. "Jackie…"

"Having second thoughts?"

"No." He rushed to assure her. The thought that she'd withdraw her offer of an affair scared him more than the no-strings-attached option. He could do this. He just had to have the right mindset. Three years ago he would have celebrated finding a woman who had no expectations from him beyond lots of orgasms. So why was he feeling conflicted now? What was it about her that scared him?

Because you've never met a woman who intrigues you, challenges you and stirs you all at the same time.

Okay, he would admit she was special. Anyone could see that. And the fact that he'd managed to break through at least the edge of her crusty outer shell was an accomplishment. He did not have to have feelings for her beyond sex.

Sex. Yeah.

Problem was, as long as they didn't make love, he could walk away unscathed. But Scott knew himself. It wasn't until after he'd done the deed with a woman those lusty feelings could turn tender.

"About this no-strings-attached thing," he murmured.

"Changing your mind?" She sounded disappointed. Both of her perceptive blue eyes were on him now. Staring straight through him as if she knew everything he was thinking.

"No, no." His penis would never forgive him if he turned back when he had such a gorgeous, willing woman on his boat. "Not backtracking."

"What is it then?"

"Shouldn't we lay down some ground rules to…" He hesitated. He didn't want to sound like an ass. "Um… prevent hurt feelings?"

She sat up, caught sight of his boner, smiled smugly.

Yes, yes, you've reduced me to my most basic instincts. Proud of yourself?

"That's sweet," she said. "But don't worry. I'm not going to fall for you."

That hurt his feelings a bit. "I was just worried about you."

"Worried that I'd fall in love with you?" She snorted.

"No one said anything about love," he retorted hastily. "But when things get intimate, people can sometimes feel possessive."

She shrugged. "Not me."

"Not ever?" He found that hard to believe.

"Nope," she said mildly. "But if ground rules make you feel better, then sure, why not. I'm fine with it. What do you have in mind?"

"I'm thinking no spending the night with each other. That can lead to increased intimacy."

"No problem. I get that. No spooning, no cuddling, no spending the entire night."

"Exactly."

She seemed unfazed by his condition. "Anything else?"

"Can we date other people?"

"Of course."

"No long, deep intimate conversations."

"No worries there on my part."

He grinned. Where had she come from? "You do realize every man fantasizes about a woman like you."

She spread her arms wide. "Your fantasy is right in front of you, Scott Everly. Stop thinking so hard and just take advantage of me."

7

I was born ready.
            —*Lieutenant Commander Scott Everly,*
                         United States Coast Guard

EXCITEMENT BUZZED Jackie's nerve endings. All her senses
were heightened. The smell of the ocean teased her nose.
Overhead, seagulls swirled, cawed. The sun dried her
hair to unruly curls and Scott's hot gaze blistered her
like a glorious sunburn.

It had been a long time since she'd felt so sexy and it
was all due to the way he looked at her. As if she were
a sea goddess just stepped from the surf and he was a
shipwrecked sailor searching for salvation.

Perfect day.

It was a perfect day until they reached the island
where Fort Jefferson stood and she spied the *Sea Anemone* anchored offshore.

What was her father doing in the Tortugas? Last she
heard he was in Bermuda.

"Hey," Scott said, "isn't that your father's boat?"

A lump of dread stuck in her throat. She hadn't seen

him in almost a year and she wasn't sure she was ready to see him now. "Yeah."

Scott beamed. "I can't wait to meet him."

"Oh, we're not going over there."

He looked startled. "What do you mean? Of course we're going over. He's your dad."

"Guess what? I know that."

A concerned expression replaced his surprise. "But wouldn't his feelings get hurt if he knew you were here and avoided him?"

Jackie laughed. "Don't worry. Nothing hurts his feelings."

The surprise was back.

She waved a hand. "Our relationship is very complicated. Let's just go have a picnic and then get out of here."

"I…" He stopped, shrugged. "Okay."

"Great, I'm starving."

He picked up the picnic basket and then extended a hand to help her out, but she ignored it. Jackie hopped into the shallow water where they'd anchored and sloshed toward the island. It was dotted with tourists who'd come to the isolated place for the interesting marine life.

"Hey, wait for me." Scott hurried to catch up.

Jackie was feeling strangely breathless and it wasn't from the exertion.

The island was flat, small and almost treeless. Fort Jefferson dominated the majority of the space. Since it was Thursday there were only a few tourists. She headed for a spot under a lone palm tree far from the *Anemone*. Obviously, it wasn't far enough. Just as Scott got the blanket spread out, a man came sauntering over.

"Jacks! Is that you? I thought that was you."

Jackie blew out her breath and glanced over to see a

blond man about her own age striding up to them. "Hello, Gary."

"You're looking…" Gary raked a gaze over her. "Radiant."

She forced a smile. "What are you doing in the Dry Tortugas?"

"I could ask you the same. Last I heard you were in Key West searching for the missing Key blenny."

She held her arms wide. "Day off."

A shocked expression lifted Gary's hay-colored eyebrows. "You? Taking a day off?" He mock staggered, clutched his heart. "It's the end of the world as we know it."

"Scott Everly," Scott said, coming over with his hand outthrust. ,

"Gary Howard." Gary shook Scott's hand. "And you are—"

"With Jackie. And who are you?" Scott draped an arm over her shoulder. It was all she could do to keep from shaking him off. What was this possessive crap he was pulling?

"Gary is my replacement." Jackie crossed her arms over her chest, the weight of Scott's arm heavy on her shoulders. "Gary, Scott is Coast Guard."

"Oh, really?" He sounded unimpressed. "I'm Jack Birchard's head research assistant."

"Speaking of the great Jack, where is Father?"

Gary's smile wavered. "He's in Paris, at the symposium on global warming."

"Ah," Jackie said. "When the cat's away the mice will play. *That's* what you're doing in the Tortugas. On your own pet project."

The guilty expression on Gary's face told her that she'd nailed it.

"Mmm…ah…well…"

"Or did he send you down here to spy on me?"

Gary snorted. "Please. You're no longer in his orbit."

That was probably true, but it still hurt to hear it. "You're not going to impress him, you know," Jackie said. "He doesn't give a damn about your independent study."

"Actually—" Gary looked like the cat who had eaten the proverbial canary "—that's what I'm counting on."

"Well, it's been nice talking to you, Gary," Jackie supplied. "Tell the old man I'm alive and feeling fine. In case he cares."

"Where are you off to?" Gary raked a gaze over her.

"We're about to have a picnic."

Gary shook his head. "Is this a sign of the apocalypse? Jackie Birchard picnicking on a day off?"

"Maybe it is," Jackie tossed over her shoulder as she walked back to the blanket under the palm tree.

"Good luck with the Key blenny," Gary called as he walked away.

Scott joined her on the blanket. "What in the hell was that all about?"

"It's nothing."

"It's obviously something. You look mad enough to eat nails."

"Then give me a sandwich so that I don't have to eat nails."

"You used to be your father's head researcher?"

"I did. Gary was his number two."

"What happened?"

"Let's see, if I remember correctly, you and I had just set up some ground rules and no intimate conversations was one of those rules."

Scott exhaled, raised his palms. "Okay. I didn't mean to stir up a hornet's nest."

"Look. I don't need for you to worry about my relationship with my father. He's not a normal guy. We're not a normal family."

"I'd sort of already figured that one out."

"Great then, let's eat. What have you got?"

He peered into the basket. "Sandwiches. Tuna fish, pimento cheese or turkey."

"I'll take the pimento cheese."

He handed her the sandwich and in the process, their fingers brushed.

The heat of contact sent a jolt of awareness shooting up her arm. She shot him a sideways glance. His eyes were half-closed, a lazy smile tipped his lips.

"Got a couple of beers." He held up two longnecks dripping with icy water. "You interested?"

"It's only noon."

"One beer. It's your day off."

"Okay." She nodded, accepted the beer he offered.

They ate in companionable silence, enjoying the moment, savoring the food and the company. Jackie's mind traveled, as it usually did, to things beneath the sea. She recalled the fish they'd seen while snorkeling. It made her feel soft and warm and happy inside.

"What are you thinking about?" Scott asked. "The jewelfish?"

She broke into a big smile, dusted sandwich crumbs from her fingers. "How did you know?"

"You might have a complex brain, Jackie Birchard, but you're not that hard to read." He glanced out at the ocean, then his gaze tracked back to rove over her bikini-clad body.

Her treacherous pulse quickened and she studied his

angular features. He looked as if he'd just tumbled out of bed, his hair wildly mussed from where it had dried on the boat ride over, his eyes sultry and suggestive.

He had an amazing body. Dressed in swim trunks and a thin white T-shirt. Rock solid. Athletic.

Her palms tingled, yearning to run over the planes of his flat belly. The spot between her legs ached for him. The fertile smell of sand and sea scented the air—potent, loamy, rich.

Scott's gaze cradled hers, desire radiating from his eyes. Her blood thickened, stirred. A slow, languid heat.

He leaned over, curved his palm around her face, leaned in for a kiss.

She did not withdraw.

He kissed her. Wild, hot and hard. A relentless force to taste and smell and feel.

Consumed.

His mouth consumed her. He plundered, conquered, possessed. The demanding flick of his tongue against hers brought a famished response so intense she felt weak, as if all her energy had been drained.

Scott groaned and locked his fingers in her hair. Kissed her harder, deeper and wilder still.

The taste of him!

He tasted like goodness and sunshine and the Fourth of July all rolled into one. Nourishing. Sturdy. Patriotic.

Jackie could not have stopped if she wanted to. She inhaled him in sweet gulps.

While the world shrank down into the width of their mouths, she opened herself up to possibilities as yet undreamed. He disarmed her completely. Her lips shuddered against his mouth and her body molded to his. In Scott's arms, she felt solidly anchored.

The sensation scared her.

She'd never wanted to be the kind of woman who locked herself into one port, one man, but why not? Her mind flirted with a dark thought. She put her palm flat against his chest and pushed back, breaking the kiss. Her lips felt swollen, bruised.

Scott's eyes were murky, lust-filled, befuddled. "What is it?"

That's when a throat-tearing scream shattered the peaceful afternoon.

INSTANTLY, SCOTT JERKED his head around to locate the source of the ear-piercing cry for help. Several yards away a woman staggered from the beach, frantically waving her arms. "Help! Help!"

The other tourists in the area froze, stared owl-eyed at the distressed woman.

Scott didn't know what was up, but he reacted instantly. *Born Ready.* In under a second, he was on his feet, racing toward the woman. His head swam a bit from shifting gears. One minute kissing Jackie, the next in Coast Guard rescue mode, but he ignored it.

The woman was blubbering incoherently, tears streaming down her round face.

"What is it?" Scott demanded, grabbing her by the shoulders.

"My son, my son! I tried to carry him, but I…" She paused, gasped for air. "Shark! Shark! A shark got him."

Shark.

That one word packed Scott's veins in ice.

The mom broke from his grip, spun around and started back toward the beach. Scott could already see a boy in the shallow tide pool, blood staining the water. The kid was pale and lay unmoving.

It did not look good.

Scott outdistanced the mother, running full-out, all the while praying that the child would not die. He sprinted over the craggy rocks, barely winced as the sharp edges poked through the soles of his thin shoes. He waded in, stumbling on the slick surface.

The child's eyes fluttered.

He was alive.

The relief that pulsed through Scott was short-lived. The boy's leg was mangled and blood flowed too quickly. An artery was involved. Time was of the essence and they were seventy miles from Key West.

Scott glanced up to see Jackie standing on the shore. "Call the Coast Guard," he said. "Ask for Carl Dugan. Tell him to send a seaplane. Now!"

Jackie nodded, her face controlled, emotionless.

Scott stripped off his shirt. The water hit him at the back of his knee. He twisted the T-shirt up, creating a makeshift tourniquet with it, and he leaned over to secure it around the thigh above where the shark had taken a vicious chunk of flesh from the boy's leg.

Amidst the bright blood staining the blue water, Scott's temple pounded as he reached down to scoop the limp boy into his arms. Poor kid. He couldn't have been more than ten.

He was vaguely aware of people ringing the shoreline. He sloshed over the rocks, slipping and tripping. Salt water splashed up, stung his eyes. Undaunted, he slogged on. When something banged into the back of his leg, Scott went tumbling forward.

The pain hit a split second later.

Sharp and jagged agony seared through his calf and knocked him to his knees. On the shore, someone screamed. He felt sticky blood bloom, and slip hotly down his own leg.

Hell's bells. He'd been bitten by a shark out in the middle of nowhere with a critically wounded child in his arms.

Coast Guard is on the way. You'll both be okay. Just get out of the water before the damn shark attacks again.

Scott forced himself to stand in spite of the pain. His leg burned and throbbed. Dammit. This was not how he'd pictured the day ending.

"He's been bitten, too!" The child's mother screamed. "Oh, my God, oh, my God. The shark got him, too!"

Great. Here he was getting cold and clammy and dizzy and he had to deal with a hysterical mother.

Scott collapsed on the shore, the kid cradled tightly against his chest. He looked up at the sky and noticed how pretty and white the clouds looked. Fluffy. Nice.

"Scott?"

A soft, calm soothing voice came from a beautiful blonde staring down at him.

"Mermaid," he croaked and reached up a finger to trace the prettiest strawberry-red lips he'd ever seen. He felt her warm hands on his leg. Inhaled her scent. Mermaids smelled so good. Not fishy at all.

"You're going to be fine. Hang on." Then the mermaid took the child from his arms. "I've got him. You can let go, Coastie."

Reality faded in and out. He heard voices, but his vision was blurry. What a wimp. Passing out over a little shark bite.

Snap out of it, Everly. Rise to the occasion. Get up.

Shark bit. He'd been shark bit.

It's not as bad as when you got shot with the harpoon. That random thought passed through his head. Because this time the mermaid was here. Everything was easier with a mermaid around.

The ground vibrated beneath him. What was this? An earthquake? Then he heard the familiar whir of helicopter blades.

Here comes the cavalry. Thank God for the Coast Guard.

"Scott, stay with me," the mermaid commanded. "You're doing fine. You saved the boy and he's going to be fine, too."

Hot dusty air blew over him. The sound of the helicopter blades grew deafening.

"Scott?"

He felt a smart sting against his cheek. The mermaid had slapped him? Who knew mermaids were so damned saucy. "Mermaid."

"You are not going under. You hear me? How embarrassing would that be? Hotshot Coast Guard done in by a little bitty bull shark?"

A trash-talking mermaid. He reached up to finger a tendril of her blond hair. The earth shook so hard he could barely breathe. The sounds of a helicopter filled his ears. He smelled motor oil. His vision dimmed.

"Scott, stay awake."

The mermaid sounded very faraway now. *Please, pretty mermaid. Don't go away. Not yet, not yet.*

For one instant he was nothing but sensation. Enveloped in sound, vibration, smell. Except for sight. He couldn't see much now. All he could see was a tunnel and at the very end a beguiling mermaid waited.

And then Scott heard nothing at all.

JACKIE FELT OUT OF PLACE in a hospital and she didn't really know what to do, but it seemed like bad form not to show up.

There hadn't been enough room for her in the helicopter what with Scott, the injured boy, the boy's mother and the medic packed onboard.

So Jackie had taken Scott's boat back to Key West, with all kinds of horrible scenarios circling in her mind. When she got to the hospital, the staff directed her to the waiting area. There she'd found a room packed with Coast Guard. She'd almost fled, but the Sector commander, Carl Dugan, had seen her and motioned her inside.

"How bad is Scott?" she asked bluntly, trying her best to tamp down the dread that had been building inside her since the incident.

"Scott's shark bite was a just bump and run," Carl said. "The shark hit his calf but didn't take any tissue. He lost a small amount of blood. Not any big deal really."

"But he lost consciousness. Surely that's cause for concern."

"Not from blood loss," Carl said. "His blood pressure dropped and he fainted. The doctor called it neurally mediated hypotension. Apparently, it's not all that uncommon an occurrence in young, healthy people. The usual triggers are standing or sitting for prolonged periods, strenuous exercise, hot weather, emotional stress, and it most frequently happens after eating a meal. It's not a condition that needs treatment."

They'd stood during the long boat ride to the Dry Tortugas. They'd scuba dived. The weather had been warm and humid. The stress of taking care of the boy and getting shark bit. They had just eaten.

"Scott fainted? That was it?" Relief pulsed through her. Scott was going to be okay.

"Yeah." The entire room rolled with laughter. "He fainted."

"Well," Carl said in Scott's defense. "There was a shark involved. It's not a pleasant experience."

"If Scott is fine, then why is everyone here?"

"We're here for the boy," Carl said. "He's in surgery. They're working to save his leg."

"What about the blood loss?"

"They had to give the boy blood, but thanks to Scott, he's going to make it. If Scott hadn't been there…" Carl left the sentence unfinished. "He's a true hero. Even if he did faint."

More snickers went around the room.

"So where's Scott?"

"In a treatment room getting examined."

"Well, if he's going to be fine…" Jackie hesitated, torn on whether to leave or stay.

"Sit down." Dugan patted the chair next to him. "He'll be happy to see you."

Jackie thought of a dozen excuses not to stay, but Dugan eyed her expectantly, so she sat. Secretly, she was glad that she could stay.

Half an hour later, a side door opened and a nurse appeared. She stood aside and Scott came through the door on crutches, a sheepish grin on his face. His right leg was wrapped up in an Ace bandage.

"He's all yours," the nurse announced.

The Coast Guard in the room jumped to their feet and saluted him as he hobbled into the waiting room.

"Sit down, knock it off," he growled sheepishly.

Several guys came over to slap him on the back and call him a hero. He shook his head, burdened by embarrassment. Midway across the floor, he stopped. His eyes lit on hers and Jackie felt an inexplicable tightening in her chest.

"I fainted," he said. "Like a little girl."

"You saved a boy's life. You have nothing to be embarrassed about."

He arched an eyebrow. "You came."

"I did."

"I didn't expect it."

"Well, if I'd known you'd just fainted..." she teased. "I brought your boat back."

"Thanks."

Just then, two women rushed into the waiting room. One was a pretty girl in her mid-twenties with hair as dark as Scott's, the other woman was older. Early fifties.

"Scotty! My poor baby." The older woman ran to him. "You scared the daylights out of us!"

Scott's face reddened. "Mom," he mumbled, tolerating her exuberant hug. "It's no big deal."

"We were in Miami when we heard," the dark-haired girl said. "Wedding shopping."

"C'mon, I'm fine."

His mother placed a palm over her heart. "After you got shot with that harpoon. After your father..." She trailed off.

"I know, I know, but everything is okay."

Jackie started inching backward. She didn't belong here. She was nothing more than Scott's potential bed buddy. She didn't want to get in the middle of a family reunion.

"Mom, Megan, there's someone I want you to meet," Scott said.

No, no, don't do this.

Feeling like a rat in a trap, Jackie forced a smile as the two women turned to see who Scott was grinning at.

"Jackie, this is my mother and my younger sister, Megan. Everyone, this is Jack Birchard's daughter, Jacqueline."

She glowered at him. *Gee, thanks for that.*

"Oh, hello," Megan said brightly and moved to extend her hand, forcing Jackie to take it. "Your father is amazing. I caught his latest documentary on PBS last week."

"He's pretty special." Jackie nodded, tight-lipped.

"What's it like having such a brilliant parent?" Scott's mother asked.

"Brilliant," Jackie echoed.

"Are you two—" Megan toggled a finger between Scott and Jackie "—seeing each other?"

"I was at the Tortugas with him when Scott fainted. I brought his boat back when he was airlifted." Jackie jerked her thumb over her shoulder. "I was just leaving."

"You were airlifted!" Scott's mother exclaimed, clucking over him like a hen over her chick.

Jackie shifted uncomfortably, gazed longingly at the door. It was just a few feet away. So close and yet so far.

Megan touched Jackie's arm. "I just had a marvelous idea. Why don't you come to our party Saturday night as Scott's plus one? It's at the aquarium. My boss is throwing my fiancé and I a belated engagement party."

"You're getting married? Congratulations."

"Next weekend. Wait…" She turned to her brother. "You can still make it to the party, can't you?"

Say no. Jackie prayed.

"Like a shark bite is going to keep me away from your engagement party," Scott scoffed.

Megan directed her beaming smile back on Jackie. "So can you make it?"

"Um, I don't know…I've got a lot of work to do and—"

"C'mon, Jackie," Scott coaxed. "It's the aquarium. Besides, I owe you. Let me make up for today."

If you owe me, let me out of this!

She mentally willed the message to him, but he didn't pick up on it. "No need," she said. "We're cool. Cucumbers."

"You've got to come," Scott's mother insisted. "You were there for my Scotty in his time of need. *I* owe you."

"I'm really busy. I'm a graduate student doing research for my doctorate and…"

"Everyone needs to take a break now and then." Scott's mother clicked her tongue.

What was it with this family and taking breaks? How did they ever get anything accomplished?

"Pretty please?" Megan coaxed.

Apparently, they weren't going to let her out of this. Her eyes met Scott's and he mouthed one word.

Sex.

Jackie fought to suppress a smile. Great. This was what she had to do to get laid?

"Yes," she relented, even though she'd rather have a root canal than go to an engagement party. It was the reward afterward that she was searching for. "I'll come."

Her gaze met Scott's again and she could have sworn he whispered, "Yes, you will."

8

Living life one wave at a time.
> —*Megan Everly, daughter and sister of Coast Guard*

IT BOTHERED JACKIE that she was looking forward to the party. In the past, parties had been nothing more than boring social obligations where she was forced to orbit her father's sun.

But now? She found herself wanting to go.

It's just because you want to see Scott again. That's all. You need to have sex with him. Put out the fire he lit so you can get your head back in your research. This is medicinal. Nothing more.

She opened her closet. It was empty. She'd brought nothing with her for the summer beyond shorts, tank tops and swimming suits.

Great. She was going to have to go shopping. The only thing she hated worse than parties.

Irritated, she trooped to the boutique on the corner and ended up with a white sundress with cutouts of sailboats along the hem. It looked good against her skin and camouflaged her skinniness.

While trying the dress on, she studied herself in the mirror. She could do with a little extra meat on her bones. It wasn't that she wanted to be so thin. She just forgot to eat much of the time, her thoughts caught up in her work. Food seemed so incidental. Something she had to remember to do.

"You're not normal," she muttered to her reflection.

"This isn't the first I'm hearing of it," her image taunted.

"Yeah, yeah. I'll always be a freak." She headed out of the dressing room with the dress tucked under her arm and almost ran into the saleswoman, who gave her a weird look. Had she overheard Jackie talking to herself?

Jackie forced a smile. "I'll take it."

"Yes, ma'am." The saleswoman rang it up.

Jackie glanced at the clock, realized that Scott would be on her doorstep within half an hour. God, what was wrong with her? How did time slip away from her so easily? Why was she so much more enamored of the Key blenny than she was of people?

She rushed back to her apartment, and once inside, she tossed the dress on the couch, stripped off her clothes and strutted naked to the shower. To her, clothes were nothing more than something to cover your body. Not something to wish for or pine over. Ah, to be a fish with no clothes to worry about at all. Just swimming nude.

Yes, but you'd have to worry constantly about being eaten.

Well, at least that was something worth worrying about. Nothing like walking the social tightrope. Jackie blew out her breath, soaped up and then rinsed off. She had just stepped out of the shower when her doorbell rang.

Scott was early.

Her heart did an irrational tap dance. What was that all about? Frowning, she wrapped a towel around her and padded to the front door.

Scott stood there looking sexy with his hair combed back off his forehead. He wore a blue shirt and beige slacks. He looked freaking delicious.

"Whoa," he laughed. "Is that what you're wearing?"

Jackie glowered. "Of course not. I'm running late. Come in."

He tracked over the threshold, glanced around at the controlled chaos.

Suddenly, Jackie saw the apartment through his eyes. The rented furniture looked worn, the room cluttered with books and notes and computer printouts and ocean-ography accoutrements. The bag from the boutique, with her dress in it, lay spread over the couch. The clothes she'd stripped out of were heaped on the floor, includ-ing her thong undies.

Jackie moved to the couch, cleared a space for him. "Have a seat. I'll be right back."

A wry smile tipped his lips. She noticed he was star-ing at the thong underwear. She bent to grab it from the floor then realized she was only wearing a towel. Ter-rific. There was no graceful way of bending over in a towel, so she left the discarded clothes where they lay.

"I'll be right back." She rushed down the hall, a heated flush spreading over her skin. She slipped into the bath-room, realized she'd left the dress in the living room. Dammit. She closed her eyes and sank against the door. She was going to have to go back in there and prove what a ditz she was.

There was a light knock on the bathroom door and her heart did that crazy tap dance again.

"Jackie?"

"Yeah?"

"Um…do you need this?"

She opened the door a crack, spied him standing there, holding the dress. She reached out, snatched it from his hand and slammed the door again. The sound of his chuckle penetrated through the cheap wooden door.

"Don't laugh at me," she hollered.

"This is really difficult for you, isn't it?"

"I'm a scientist," she grumbled, dropping the towel and pulling the sundress over her head. "Not a party maven."

"Relax, mermaid. You're going to be just fine. No expectations. Let's just have a good time."

"Easy for you to say," she muttered.

Okay. Now she had the dress on, but her bra was in the living room and she was sans panties and Everly was standing right outside the door. She was flat chested. She could get away without the bra, but she wasn't going to go out without any underwear. She wasn't some tarty Hollywood starlet.

Makeup. Get some makeup on and then you can grab a pair of panties before you leave the bedroom.

She glanced at the sparse makeup case on her counter. She had one tube of lipstick and another of mascara and they both were probably at least a year old.

Who cared? Right? She never pretended to be a beauty queen. She rolled on the lipstick. A soft peach color that enhanced her tan. Not bad. People wouldn't throw up when she walked by. Then she brushed on the ebony mascara. It made her eyes look instantly bigger. Fine. Good. That was enough primping. She dropped the mascara into the makeup bag and zipped it closed.

Taking a deep breath, she wrenched opened the door. Scott was standing right there with an ocean-size grin on his face, and his muscular arms crossed over his chest, looking all hot and manly.

Oh, wow.

She startled at his proximity and all the air leaked from her lungs in a slow, soft hiss. Hair. She'd forgotten to deal with her hair. She was the worst girlie-girl on the planet. She reached up and yanked the ponytail holder from her hair, ran a hand through her locks to fluff them. That had to do.

"Wow," Scott said, his gaze traveling over her body. "You look awesome."

Jackie blew a raspberry. "You don't have to lie."

A roguish expression lit his eyes. "I am not lying. You underestimate your beauty, Jackie Birchard."

She waved a hand. "Who cares about looks? They don't last. What lasts is a sharp mind."

"You have absolutely nothing to worry about on that score, either."

She cocked her head, evaluated him through narrowed eyes. "Where are your crutches?"

"I ditched them. They just slowed me down."

"And you felt like a dork using them."

"Yeah," he admitted. "All I've got is shark teeth track marks on my calf."

"Those pretty legs are ruined. It's a travesty."

"I thought you didn't care about looks."

"My looks," she teased. "Boy toys have an image to maintain."

"Oh, so that's how you see me. A boy toy."

"Okay, a misnomer I'll grant you." She raked her gaze over him, grinned impishly. "I stand corrected. Man toy."

"Ready?" He cocked his head in the direction of her front door. She was very aware that her bedroom stretched out behind her, just as messy as her living area.

"I don't normally do parties," she fretted, pulling her bedroom door closed behind her.

"I figured that."

"All I have to say is that you better be really good in bed, Everly." She stopped to pick up her purse. A sensible black bag that matched everything. Except her simple white dress and white sandals. She peered down at her feet. Mother of pearl, she should have gotten a pedicure.

"I am." He grinned.

"You're smug. Don't think I'm kidding." She picked up her house keys, dropped them into her inappropriate handbag. She couldn't have sex with him. What was she talking about? She hadn't waxed. What was she? A woman or a surfboard? "I expect peak performance even with your shark bite."

"Flesh wound."

"And no fainting."

"You sure know how to hit a guy where it hurts, mermaid."

"Why do you keep calling me that?"

"Because you belong to the sea."

She had no comeback for that. When he was right, he was right.

"Nicknames border on romance. This isn't romance. That's what we agreed. This is about sex."

"Ah, come on, you can't indulge my sexual fantasies a little while?" He jingled his change in his pockets while she locked the front door.

She straightened, met his seductive gaze. "And what might that fantasy be?"

"Mermaids," he whispered huskily. "I've always wanted to get it on with a mermaid."

An effervescent laugh rolled from her throat. Giggling? She was giggling? She'd never giggled in her life.

Well, you're giggling now.

"I might be persuaded to indulge in some role-playing fantasies," she told him as she headed down the steps ahead of him. "As long as you don't mind being Neptune."

"Three-prong trident? What's not to love?"

This, Jackie decided, was going to be a lot of fun.

It was only when they were in the car and on their way to the aquarium that she realized she'd forgotten to put on underwear.

SCOTT DROVE TOWARD the aquarium, uncertainty pushing against him. What was he doing here with this woman? Clearly, she wanted nothing more than to use him to sate her sexual appetites and he was taking her to his sister's engagement party. Why?

What's so wrong with a casual affair? Isn't it better that you know where you stand with her? No expectations. No hurt feelings. You're not exactly looking for happily-ever-after, either. And hey, it's been six months without sex. Take whatever she can give and let it be enough.

Right. Yes. It made sense. Why then did he feel so damned unsettled by the thought?

When he pulled into the aquarium's parking lot, she reached out and touched his shoulder. "Wait."

He felt her touch clean to his bones. What was that all about? Slowly, he turned to look at her. She was so beautiful it hurt his head. "What is it?"

"I need a moment to prep for this."

"What are you so worried about? It's not like you're my girlfriend or anything."

"I just need to bolster my courage."

"This is really difficult for you." That surprised him.

She was so self-possessed. He couldn't imagine any-thing upsetting her equilibrium and here she was ner-vous about something he took for granted. A party. Why would a party make her nervous?

"Because," she said, accurately reading his mind. "A party is not a natural environment for a mermaid."

"Ah, but the party is in an aquarium," he pointed out. "You should feel right at home."

"All right." She exhaled, gave him a shaky smile. "I'm ready."

Scott unbuckled his seat belt and got out. He tried to rush around to open the passenger-side door for her, but she was already popping out before he got there.

She pointed a finger at him. "No, no, none of that gentlemanly stuff, Everly. We're just planning on being sex buddies. I'm here because your sister invited me and I couldn't think of a way to get out of it. Besides I'm a sucker for aquariums."

He settled a hand to the small of her back, leaned in to whisper in her ear. "Liar. You're here because you want to be with me."

"I want to have sex with you," she corrected.

"Same thing."

"Whatever."

"You are a contrary woman."

"Apparently you like that about me."

"Apparently I do," he said, mildly surprised to realize it was true. He enjoyed bantering with her. "C'mon."

He guided her into the aquarium.

"And the fish," she said. "I came for the fish."

"Me, too. I like them as much as you do."

"Doubtful."

"You don't own a patent on liking fish."

"How do you know? I might. I am Jack Birchard's daughter."

"Oh, I knew this was going to happen eventually." He winked. "Playing the celebrity card."

"Like you don't play the Coast Guard card when it's handy," she quipped.

"Scott! Jackie!" Megan spotted them and broke away from the pack of people she'd been talking to and came over to greet them. She took them around the room, introducing them. "Here you are, big brother, living life one wave at a time."

It was a Coast Guard expression their father used to say when life was going well. The civilian equivalent was along the lines of "enjoy the moment."

"And this wave is fine," he replied smoothly.

"He's incorrigible," Megan said to Jackie. "You have to know that." She switched her gaze back to Scott. "Surely, she knows that."

"I know that." Jackie nodded.

"And yet you like him anyway. There's hope for you yet, big brother."

"Shoo, go, preside over your event." He tickled Megan in the ribs. She laughed and darted away.

Scott knew most of the people at the party. Jackie, in spite of her proclamation of not being a people person, handled the crowd with aplomb. She shook hands and listened while others made small talk and she wasn't too obvious when she kept sliding wistful glances at fish tanks. He knew that's where her head was. Swimming around in the water.

He smiled.

People kept asking him about the shark attack. He told them how the boy was doing, deflecting attention off his own wound. They called him a hero. He refused the title. He was Coast Guard. Saving lives was his job. Dave, his brother-in-law-to-be, teased him about fainting. He'd expected some razzing and he took it like a man. He'd rather be razzed than dubbed a hero.

His leg ached where the shark's teeth had branded him, but he ignored it. He was Coast Guard. He could deal with a little pain. Especially when he had Jackie to look at, and that took his mind off the minor discomfort.

They ate appetizers on tiny plates—mini spinach quiches, bacon-wrapped shrimp, guacamole on blue corn tortilla chips. And then out came the champagne. Whitley Montgomery, Megan's boss and the head of the aquarium, toasted Megan and Dave and gave a brief speech. The crowd applauded and cheered.

Then Whitley paused. "I've just learned we have a special guest here tonight, as well. I want you all to give a warm welcome to the renowned Jack Birchard's daughter, Jackie."

Jackie's face flushed and she ducked her head.

"We're so happy to have you in Key West." He raised his glass and proposed a toast to Jackie.

A forced smile crossed her face and she shifted her weight from foot to foot. Scott could see she was uncomfortable with the attention.

"I've met your father," Whitley said. "He's an amazing man."

"Yes." Jackie's face tightened. "He is."

Scott knew a bit about what it was like living in the shadow of a legend. You always felt like you could never really measure up no matter how hard you tried. That you had somehow let the world down by not being as accomplished as your parent. But Jackie had to deal with that feeling on a whole different level.

His father had been killed in the line of duty and as a

result, Scott felt like he had to keep his father's memory alive by the way he behaved. Honor his father. But Jackie's dad was world famous. Here in Key West, Scott lived in his father's shadow, but in D.C., he was his own man. Jackie could never escape the reach of her father's legend. Sympathy took hold of him and all he wanted to do was help her escape scrutiny for an evening.

Whitley had cornered Jackie and was heartily extolling her father's virtues.

Scott moved toward her. "Whitley, can I steal Jackie away from you for a minute?"

"Oh, sure, sure. I didn't mean to hog her. She's just so fascinating to talk to." Whitley gazed at Jackie with puppy-dog admiration. "I hope you'll consider speaking at one of our lecture series."

"I'll give it some thought. It's been nice speaking with you, Mr. Montgomery."

"Better yet, ask your father. We'd love to have *him* do the lecture series."

Jackie had an undiplomatic, *dream on, buster,* expression on her face. "I'll let him know."

Scott took her elbow and guided her away. "You're doing well. Don't pop him one in the mouth."

"I wasn't going to." She chuckled. "But it did cross my mind."

"Consider yourself rescued. Let's get out of here."

"Thank you," she breathed. "I never know how to get away in these situations. I usually end up saying I have to go to the bathroom and then I head for the nearest exit."

"I've got your back, mermaid. This time I'm leading you out the nearest exit." He guided her down a long, darkened hallway.

"Where are we going?" She hung on to his arm.

Just that simple taking of his arm had Scott's temperature boiling. "Behind the scenes."

"Oh?" She sounded intrigued.

He paused in front of a door that had a combination lock on it. He punched in the numbers.

"How do you know the combination?"

"I've been here with Megan."

"She told you the combination?"

"I'm observant." The door clicked as the tumblers fell into place. Grinning, he pushed it open.

"Hey, if this Coast Guard thing doesn't pan out, you have a promising career in breaking and entering."

They were in a cement tunnel that led to the inner workings of the aquarium.

"We're on the inside looking out." Glee edged Jackie's voice. "The guests are out there, we're in here and they can't see us."

"Viewing the world from the fishes' point of view."

"Something I've spent my life trying to do," she said.

"You like it better on this side of the glass, don't you?"

She nodded, peered at the parrot fish swimming past them in dizzy circles. "This *is* fun. Thank you."

"You're easy to please." He tucked her closer to his side and experienced a heady sense of promise when she didn't pull away.

They wandered by a tank filled with small, colorful fish. Near the bottom, amidst sand, colored gravel and sea grass, a pair of sea horses was engaged in a courtship ritual. They swam side by side, tails entwined. The sea horse equivalent of holding hands. Slowly, in unison, they moved in a languid waltz.

"It's called the predawn dance," Jackie murmured.

"I know." He leaned in closer, caught a sweet whiff of her lime-scented hair. "My sister works here."

"Sorry." She smiled. "When I'm with laymen I assume they don't know anything about marine biology."

"I know much more than you think I do," he remarked. "Sea horses are monogamous," Scott added, not knowing why the hell he said that.

"Actually," Jackie corrected, "that's a common myth. While many sea horses form bonding pairs that last a season, it's not an until-death-do-us-part union. And many species readily switch partners whenever the opportunity arises. *H. abdominalis* and *H. breviceps* have even been observed breeding in groups."

"Orgy-loving sea horses? Who knew?"

"Me, for one." Jackie laughed. The sound, in the confines of the back room, seemed to project into the future, beckoning tomorrow.

"You don't have a romantic bone in your body, do you?" he joked.

"Male sea horses gestate the babies. That's pretty romantic in my book."

"Why do the males gestate the babies? In the grand scheme of things, that's pretty unique."

"Are you sure you want to know? It blows the romantic notion."

"In the interest of keeping our relationship strictly biological, sure. We don't need no stinkin' romance."

She rewarded him with a wide grin. "Well, Bateman's principle suggests—"

"What? Bateman? Who's that?"

"In biology, Bateman's principle is a theory that suggests females expend more energy in the production of offspring than males and therefore, females are a limiting resource."

"In other words, eggs are more valuable than sperm."

Her eyes sparkled. "Exactly. So in regard to sea

horses, if Bateman's theory holds true, then the fact that the male gestates the offspring suggests that generating the eggs drains more from the female than gestating the eggs does for the male. A recent study determined that the energy burden on the female was exactly double that of what the male expended in gestation."

Scott shook his head. "Boy, you sure know how to shatter a good romantic story."

"Science is science. It's about facts. Not fairy tales." She wandered away from him, her gaze going to the tank filled with sharks.

The bite marks underneath the Ace bandage on Scott's leg throbbed, but he followed her anyway.

Jackie watched the sharks for a while, and then hugged herself. "I love it in here. Thank you for rescuing me."

"Thank *you*," he emphasized.

"What for?"

"If you hadn't agreed to come to the party, Megan would have found someone to fob off on me. Now that she's found Dave she hates that's I'm single and she loves playing matchmaker. Just FYI."

Jackie smiled. "You're welcome, and thanks for the heads-up."

Her smile beguiled him and Scott couldn't resist moving even closer. He reached out, took her firm little chin between his fingers. He tipped her face up. She peered at him as if she held the secrets to the underwater universe. Hell, she probably did.

Her smile widened.

God, she looked so beautiful when she smiled.

Scott dipped his head and pressed his lips to hers, and felt her smile spread from ear to ear. Her wicked little tongue flicked out and traced over his lips in a glorious vibration that drove straight down to his burgeoning erection.

"Jackie," he murmured and pulled her to his chest.

She wrapped her arms around his neck.

He pressed his face against her hair, smelled the lovely scent of her. She smelled like home. Key West. Gardenia, lime and sea. "Jackie."

Her nipples beaded hard against his chest.

"You're not wearing a bra," he said huskily, his body going hard instantly.

"I'm not wearing any underwear, either," she whispered.

Instantly, his balls drew up hard and tight against his body. "Hot damn, woman, what are you trying to do to me?"

"Same thing you're doing to me, sailor."

"I want you."

"I know." A lusty light shone in her eyes.

Fish tanks surrounded him. Dolphins and sharks. Sea urchins and sea horses. Starfish and clown fish. Music filtered in through the sound system. "Oceans" by The Format. This felt so right. Perfect.

Her hand went to his belt buckle.

He reached for the top button at her cleavage.

"Protection?" she murmured.

"Don't worry. I've got your back."

"Where?"

"Hip pocket of my pants."

"You were ready."

"Mermaid, I was born ready."

"Lucky me."

"No more talking. Let's just let nature take its course."

"Okay." Her hands reached to the hem of her dress

and she stripped it over her head. Then, just like that, she stood totally naked in front of him.

Scott just thought he'd been hard before. Seeing her lithe form backlit by the aquarium lights yanked the air right from his lungs. "Jackie."

"Scott."

"You're incredible."

"And I'm naked and you're not. That's not fair."

She didn't have to ask twice.

Scott fumbled for his belt, whipped it off, unzipped his pants.

She laughed, danced away from him like a saucy sea horse. Making him work for it.

"Where are you going?" he wheedled.

"Can't make this too easy for you. Come and get me if you think you can handle it."

She dodged around a bin where they stored fish food, her blond hair streaming out behind her. She looked exactly like a mermaid. He swallowed a gulp of emotion, stripped off his shirt, while at the same time kicking off his shoes.

"C'mere," he intoned.

She stuck out her tongue, ducked behind an aqua tank, out of his sight.

He pulled a condom from his back pocket before he took off his pants along with his BVDs. His heart pounded extraordinarily hard and he couldn't remember the last time he'd been this aroused.

Where was she? He could hear her moving down the tunnel.

"Here fishy, fishy," he cajoled, opening the condom and rolling it on as he searched. He moved into another room that held more aquariums.

It was incredibly arousing to realize that on the other

side of those thick tanks that people were mingling at the party. The fish and the water vegetation, the darkness in the back, contrasting with the lighting in the main room, would prevent anyone from seeing them back here, but still the possibility they were semipublic spurred his adrenaline.

He heard a giggle, spun around.

She was behind him.

How had she gotten behind him?

He pivoted, dived for her.

She ran.

He missed. "Naughty mermaid. Get back here and take what's coming to you."

He returned to the room he'd just left. She was nowhere in sight. He touched his cock. It was beyond granite. "Where are you?"

Another glorious giggle erupted.

It lifted his heart to hear her having a good time. She didn't often have a good time and to think that he was an instrument of her pleasure puffed his chest with pride. "Oh, Jackie, where are you?"

He peered behind the aqua tank, and then felt a light tickling on his bare ass. He snaked his hand around, grabbed her wrist. "Gotcha."

She squealed.

He turned to face her.

"You're pretty quick for a shark-bit man."

His leg was hurting from the activity but he didn't care. No pain, no gain, right? His leg was still in the Ace bandage. It would keep him secure.

She wriggled in his grip. Her eyes were wide, her lips glistening. Her breasts rose and fell in a perky rhythm as she sucked in air.

"You're mine now, you little mammal."

"Not if I swim away."

"You're not going anywhere." He pulled her to him.

She trembled with excitement and her excitement fired his. He couldn't say what came over him, but it was powerful as the ocean waves. Timeless and ferocious. He pushed her backward until her spine flattened against the tank. Instantly, she raised her legs, wrapped them around his waist.

And then he was in her. He didn't know how it happened. One minute they were peering into each other's eyes and the next minute his red-hot rod slipped into her juicy wetness and he just sank into her. They both expelled air-hungry groans.

His mouth captured hers. *Blow my mind.* Man, she was the sweetest thing he'd ever tasted. He moved in her and the world spun out of control.

Her fingernails dug into his back. His calf cried out, cursing him, but pain was nothing compared to the exquisite feeling surging through his body. He ground his hips, pushing her against the wall.

"Harder," she cried.

He gave her what she wanted. Her head bounced against the glass.

"Yes, yes!" she cried. "Harder, faster. Give me all you've got, Scott."

He sank into her as deeply as he could go, pumping his hips, thrusting fast and hard. He went blind. He couldn't see anything. All he could do was smell the musky scent of their joining. Feel the tangle of her hair flowing over his face. Taste the salt of her skin. Hear her high sweet keening.

"Yes, oh, yes. I'm close. Don't stop, don't stop."

He couldn't have stopped if he wanted to. He drove into her in a way he'd never driven into any woman.

With full, complete abandon. He blew through her like a hurricane, came in a white-hot gush and immediately regretted his hair-trigger response.

Their first joining was over far too soon.

9

You have to go out, no one says you have to
come back.
> —*Common saying among the Coast Guard
> rank and file*

THEY RESTED ON THE CEMENT floor, still on the backside of
the aquarium. Jackie threaded her hand through Scott's
lush dark hair. Sweat glistened over his back. She traced
her fingers over his spine, his head lying facedown in her
lap. She tracked down his sculpted butt—his incredible,
amazing butt—to his firm, muscular legs.

Then she saw blood staining the Ace bandage around
his right calf. "You're bleeding."

"I know."

"Why didn't you stop?"

"What's a little blood when you're flying high on sex
endorphins."

"It's going to hurt when the endorphins wear off."

"Don't care." He kissed her inner thigh.

She laughed, wriggled. "That tickles."

"How about this?" His tongue traveled down.

"You're incorrigible."

"Hmm." He planted more kisses over her skin. "I could get real used to this taste."

She made a small, unintended noise, and she was uncertain what it meant.

He raised his head. Looking at him was like staring at the sun. Too bright to be endured for long. Hot. Intense. The source of stark, blistering energy. He cracked her heart as wide-open as the Atlantic Ocean and that worried her.

"Are you ready to go again?" he asked, thankfully bringing things back to sex.

"Better question, are you?"

"I haven't had sex in six months. So, yeah. I'm ready to go again."

"You have a rapid recovery time," she said.

"Why thank you for noticing."

"Do you have another condom?" she dared.

He sat up. "Just let me find my pants."

He got to his feet. She noticed he was careful not to put too much weight on his right leg. A pinprick of guilt passed through her. This wasn't fair to him. He was in pain.

"Scott…"

"Yes?" He retrieved his pants, dug in the pocket.

"Forget it…you're hurt."

"You don't get it, do you? I'm Coast Guard. Pain is part of life."

"But I don't want to be the cause of your pain."

"You didn't bite my leg." He came back to her, his erection bouncing proudly. He was ready again. Jackie grinned.

"I love to see you smile." He reached a hand down to her.

She placed her palm in his and he pulled her to her feet.

"So forget about my leg. Tell me what you want."

"My turn to look at the fishes while we do it," she said.

And to keep from looking into your eyes when you make love to me.

Looking into his face when they were entangled was too intimate. It bordered on something more than sex, and she didn't want to go there. She was not going to lead this man on. Even though she'd made it clear their relationship could be nothing more than sex, she knew things would get complicated if emotions got involved, and staring each other in the eyes punched emotional buttons that shouldn't be pushed.

"If that's what you want." He kissed her.

He was the best kisser. Firm and warm. Not too wet. Not too dry. Just the right amount of moisture. She swallowed him up. *Yes.*

In an instant, she felt her body respond. Speaking of moisture. She was immediately ready for him all over again.

She broke off the kiss, turned and planted both palms against the tank. "There are people on the other side of this tank."

"I know."

"They're out there talking and drinking and laughing and we're in here—"

He said a dirty word that made her ears burn and her cheeks heat.

"Yeah," she purred lustily. "We're doing that."

His hands went around her waist. He pressed his body against hers. His erection was hot steel against her buttocks.

"Spread your legs," he said.

She did as he asked, spreading her legs wide while

she watched the sea horses. They were mating, too. Entangled with each other, but anchored to nothing else. Snout-to-snout they drifted upward out of the sea grass, spiraling upward as they rose. In spite of her scientific training and knowledge, Jackie saw it now as a beautiful, romantic dance of love.

Scott's fingers trailed down her back to her buttocks. He tickled her lightly, then moved on down. His hand slipped between her legs and her body shivered involuntarily as he lightly touched the sweet hood that offered so much pleasure.

"Mmm," he murmured then leaned forward to plant kisses along her spine.

Jackie moved against him, reveling in the sensations sweeping her away. She watched the fish, felt his tongue, smelled the scent of their bodies, heard the sound of his rough masculine breathing, tasted her own desire floating hot and heady in her mouth.

His fingers stayed busy, strumming, rubbing, caressing. Touching her in ways that unfurled her. She bloomed. In his hands, she was a rosebud in the sun. Opening, softening, exploding with rich fragrance.

She closed her eyes, pressed her face against the cool glass. It was the next-best thing to being underwater.

The tip of him pushed lightly at her entrance. He stopped. Just stayed there for a moment. His throbbing erection bobbing against her.

Come in, come in so we can come together.

She pushed back against him, causing him to enter her.

"Minx," he whispered against her ear.

"Stop teasing."

He gently gathered a handful of her hair in his hand. "Let's mate like the sea horses, mermaid."

She pushed harder and he was in her to the hilt. He tugged on her hair. Not too hard. Just the right amount of tension to let her know he was fully in control. She liked it. Giving up control. Letting him take over in this context.

With one hand on her hair and the other clamped to her waist, he started gyrating his hips, pushing her forward. She opened her eyes, staring into the tank. He was long and hard and it felt so good having him buried deep within her. She couldn't have escaped if she wanted to. She didn't want to. She liked this. Liked what he was doing to her. Liked him.

Hell, she liked him.

He's inside of you. It's probably a good thing that you like him.

But she couldn't like him too much. She had to draw a line.

Before she could fully develop that thought, he quickened the tempo. Tugging her hair, riding her hard, pushing her over the edge again. She hadn't even realized she was ready to tumble, but suddenly, her knees were weak and her body filled with an ocean full of sensation. Rippling, undulating, waving.

He was dragging her overboard. Taking her down to depths she'd never before dived, darkly mysterious and sweetly scary.

The orgasm hit so hard she almost choked on the scream she tried to bite back. People might not able to see them on the other side of the tank, but if she screamed, they would surely hear her.

He held her as she trembled, sinking to the ground with her in his arms and Jackie had to admit it was the best sex she'd ever experienced.

THEY GOT DRESSED, tried to tamp down the smirks of pleasure on their faces and edged back to the party. Scott reached out to take her hand, but Jackie pretended she didn't see him extend it.

"Look," she said, shifting her gaze to the aquarium. "A red-and-white-striped filefish."

Scott came up behind her. She could feel his breath against the top of her head. He rested his hands on her shoulders. "You doin' okay?"

"Fine." She turned back to him, forced a smile. "Never better."

"Scotty!" Megan exclaimed. "There you are. We were wondering where you'd gotten off to. I've got someone I want you to meet." Megan linked her arm through her brother's. "You don't mind if I borrow him, do you, Jackie?"

"He's a free man." Jackie laughed, waved a hand.

Scott shot her an unfathomable look.

Feeling breathless, Jackie turned away, pulse fluttering in her throat. She needed air and perspective. While Megan hauled Scott away, she slipped out the exit door.

Once free, she rested her back against the cool stone of the outside of the building and looked up into the sky filled with twinkling stars. Why did she feel so...so... What was she feeling?

Her body sweetly ached and she was sated in a way she hadn't been sated in a very long time and yet something was off-kilter. She couldn't put her finger on it. Couldn't name it, but the anxiety was there. A knot constricting her solar plexus.

The breeze ruffled her skirt and she took in a big gulp of air and closed her eyes. Her limbs tingled pleasantly. This was good. Right?

"I see you made good your escape." Scott's voice came to her from the dark.

She opened her eyes, met his smile. "Crowded in there."

"You don't have to explain yourself to me."

"I—"

"Needed some distance," he finished for her.

She nodded.

"Are you ready for me to take you home?"

"Would that be rude? I have so much work to do."

"No problem at all." His smile was still in place, but he sounded disappointed.

"Thank you."

"You hungry? We burned up a lot of calories back there."

"We did."

"It doesn't have to be anything fancy. Fish taco from a beach vendor."

"That sounds perfect," she said, quelling the panicky sensation urging her to tell him to take her straight home. Yes, they were using each other for sex, but that didn't mean she had to be rude about it and she *was* hungry.

"C'mon." He offered his hand.

This time, she took it and he led her across the parking lot to the rental sedan he picked her up in.

She paused. "Um...I'm not good at this social stuff, but I just realized I should probably go say goodbye to your mother and sister."

"I already did it for you."

"You knew I was ready to go," she said, feeling relieved and grateful.

"You're not as enigmatic as you think you are, Jackie Birchard."

"Or you're just pretty astute, Lieutenant Commander Everly."

"There is that." He opened the door for her.

She slid in, smoothing down her skirt as she went. He closed the door and walked around to the driver's side.

"What kind of car do you drive?" she asked. "Back in D.C."

"Guess."

She canted her head and studied him. "Some kind of sports car. Low slung, red and fast."

"Nope."

"Then something rugged and outdoorsy. Jeep?"

"Nope."

"You don't drive a sedan."

"Nope."

"Pickup truck?"

"Nope."

"Prius?"

"That's what *you* drive."

"How do you know that? You've never seen my car."

"I'm observant, Miss Ecology. I saw the key on your coffee table."

"So what *do* you drive?"

"It gets good gas mileage. But it does go fast."

Jackie frowned. "I have no idea."

"Ducati."

"A motorcycle. You drive a motorcycle. Of course, why didn't I expect it? Sleek and dangerous. In hindsight it is so obvious. I told you I was clueless about people."

"You're not as clueless as you like to pretend. I'm guessing your father rewarded you for introversion and discouraged social activities."

"He's pretty dismissive of most people," she admitted.

"The only way into his inner circle is through a high IQ and a serious penchant for the ocean."

"I like the ocean," Scott said.

"You're also smart."

"Not Mensa quality."

"Neither am I. My father was so disappointed when he had me tested when I was a kid and discovered I had an IQ of only a 138."

"Sounds pretty damn smart to me."

"Won't get me into Mensa and my father has an IQ of 180. So in his book, I'm slow."

"And with the social skills of a sea cucumber?"

"You said it, I didn't." Jackie laughed.

"You have a great laugh," Scott said. "You need to use it more often."

"I'll keep that in mind."

They both drew in simultaneous breaths that echoed strangely in the confines of the car. Jackie cast a nervous glance outside the window. The moon was bright, three-quarters full.

Scott pulled up into beach area parking not far from her apartment. Even at nine o'clock at night the beach was still hopping with tourists. Colorful lights were strung over the pier and through the palm trees. At a nearby pavilion people danced as a live band played "Ocean Size Love."

"Can you dance?" Scott asked.

"Seriously?"

"I take that as a no. Tell you what, you can hold on to my belt loop while I waltz you across the dance floor."

She shrugged, feeling sheepish. "I'd rather not."

"Is it me or the dancing?"

"I'm not the most graceful woman in the world."

"You underestimate yourself."

"And you've never seen me dance."

"Expand your world, Jackie. Come out of the ocean for a while."

She wrinkled her nose. "Dancing is too romantic."

"Last chance for a first dance," he wheedled.

"That doesn't make any sense. If I ever dance with you that will be our first dance."

"Last chance for tonight," he amended.

"We've got rules, remember."

He paused, splayed a palm to the back of his neck. "Yeah, you're right." Except he looked a little wounded.

"How about a stroll on the beach?"

She should say no, but she was a sucker for water. "Now you're speaking my language."

They took their time walking along the beach. Jackie took off her sandals and dug her toes in the sand. The wind ruffled the hem of her dress. Just a short time ago she'd been naked with Scott in the back of the aquarium. She dipped her head, pressed her lips together. The sound of the ocean was a lullaby, whispering sweet nothings as it rolled up and back.

How many nights had she fallen asleep on the *Sea Anemone* listening to this sound? Jackie hugged herself.

"You're cold," Scott observed.

"No." She smiled.

"What are you grinning about?"

"The ocean. The moon." She waved. *You.*

He stepped closer. His eyes gleamed. He looked like he wanted to eat her up in a very good way.

Staring at him was too intense. So she danced away, arms outstretched, and pirouetted across the sand behind him. What was this feeling spreading through her like hot chocolate on a cold morning?

His chuckle rang out. "And you said you couldn't dance."

She turned her head to slant him a coy glance and noticed a dark stain on his pants at the calf of his right leg. "You're bleeding."

"What?"

"Your leg. It's bleeding." She moved closer.

He muttered a mild curse.

"Come on," she said, linking her arm through his.

"Where?"

"To my apartment."

He wriggled his eyebrows. "I like the sound of that."

"To doctor your leg," she clarified.

"You have a first aid kit?"

"All good oceanographers carry a first aid kit. The sea can be dangerous."

"All good Coast Guards carry a first aid kit, as well."

"What do you know," she teased. "We have something in common."

"The ocean. First aid kits. Next thing you know people will be calling us soul mates."

She dropped her arm from his.

"Sorry. I was kidding. I didn't mean that the way it sounded. That was too romantic, wasn't it?"

She paused, her heartbeat strangely rapid. She should correct him right now. Tell him that yes, it was far too romantic to say such a thing to her. But instead she found herself saying, "I'll let it slide. This time."

They walked the rest of the way to her apartment in silence. Once inside, she tossed her purse and sandals on the floor beside the door. "Have a seat. I'll be right back."

She scurried to the bathroom, grabbed the first aid

kit and rushed back to find Scott studying her computer monitor.

"Wow," he said. "This is high-tech. I'm impressed."

"Property of the University of California. One of the reasons I was ticked off when you pulled up my equipment."

"Direct satellite feed and everything."

She scratched her cheek. "What can I say? Being Jack Birchard's daughter does have some perks. Now take off your pants."

"You can be a bit bossy." The corners of his eyes crinkled in amusement.

"I'm direct, not bossy. Drop your trousers."

"You don't have to ask me twice." He unsnapped his pants with a lazy smile, slid the zipper down.

Her helpless gaze followed his movements and her thoughts instantly returned to the aquarium. *Stop it. He's hurt. The last thing he needs is more sex.*

But when he shucked off his shoes and pants she could see he was getting hard again. She averted her eyes from his BVDs. "Lie down on the couch."

He settled onto his back, stretched out.

"On your stomach," she commanded. She couldn't keep staring at his erection barely cloaked behind thin cotton and not do something about it. *Come on, three times in one evening is a bit excessive, don't you think?*

"You'd make a good drill sergeant. Ever thought about joining the Coast Guard?" he drawled.

"Do you want this wound dressed or not?"

"I can think of something else—"

"Everly!"

"Okay, okay." He turned over.

She could see the outline of his magnificent butt. *Stop looking at his ass! Get busy.*

With studied purpose, she turned to tending his wound. As a scientist, she wasn't particularly alarmed at the jagged kerf. But as his lover—yes, she *was* his lover and that thought brought a heated flush to her skin—she experienced a tug of sympathy in the pit of her stomach. The teeth marks weren't excessive, but he would forever bear the scar of their first date. He could never forget her no matter how hard he tried. He was marked. One day, he'd tell his future wife the story of how he went scuba diving with Jack Birchard's daughter and by the end of the afternoon he'd been shark bit.

Or maybe not. Maybe he would leave her out of the story altogether and just talk about rescuing the boy. For no good reason, the thought of being left out of his future narrative saddened Jackie.

She cleaned the wound with peroxide and then bandaged it up again. "I'd tell you to stay off it for a few days but I have a feeling you wouldn't listen to me."

Scott sat up, looked down to admire her handiwork. "You're right. I'm not one to sit around, but thanks for this."

"Don't mention it." She dealt with putting away the supplies to keep busy. He didn't make any move to put his pants on. Where was this going?

They stood looking at each other; neither one of them said anything, but the air fairly crackled with tension.

Then thankfully, miraculously, the phone rang. The caller ID flashed her professor's number. "I have to take this," she said.

"Sure, sure." He finally reached for his pants as she snatched up the phone and turned her back.

"Hello."

"Jackie, Professor Donnelly here."

"Is something up?"

"I didn't receive your weekly report and I'm just calling to check in. You're never late with your assignments and since you're out there on your own, I worried."

Stunned, Jackie gulped. In her flustered state over her date with Scott, she'd forgotten to send her report. It was prepared. Ready to be emailed, she'd just forgotten to press Send. Was she that thrown off balance? "I'm so sorry. The date slipped my mind."

"It's no problem really. Like I said, it was so uncharacteristic of you that I got concerned."

"I'll email it to you right now, Professor Donnelly, and I promise this will never happen again." She had never missed a deadline and she was mortified to have done so now.

This is what happens when you let sex take over your brain.

"No worries. Now that I know you're all right, I'm happy."

"Thanks for checking up on me," Jackie said, then rang off.

"Troubles?" Scott asked.

"I've been neglecting my work." She cradled the receiver.

"Because of me."

"I try not to blame others for my mistakes." She pushed a hand through her hair.

They studied each other across the length of the room. The expression on Scott's face said he wanted to scoop her into his arms and take her to bed. The pounding in Jackie's chest said she wanted the same thing.

She wasn't going to go there. Scott was sexy as all get out and she really enjoyed herself with him, but this was her career, her livelihood, her life. He was nothing except a good-looking distraction.

"I should go," he said.

She didn't argue.

He moved toward the door. "Thanks again for the nursing care."

"You're welcome."

He opened the door, turned back at the threshold.

Just go.

Jackie planted one bare foot against the side of her opposite leg, stood like a stork. She forced a smile and tried not to think too hard. "Have a good night."

"When can I see you again?"

"We should cool it for a while. I have a lot of work to do."

"I understand." He shook his head and Jackie realized he didn't understand at all.

Neither did she.

"I guess I'll see you when I see you?" he asked.

"I'll give you a call in a few days."

"Do you have my number?"

"No."

"Give me your cell and I'll program it in."

"Just tell me. I can do it."

He clenched his jaw, and then told her his number. "Will you remember it?"

"Yes," she told him, but she knew she would not. Better to forget him now before she got in any deeper. It had been a fun night, but it was over. She had to get back on track. Had to recommit to what was the most important thing in her life.

And it wasn't Scott.

10

Sun over foreyard.
—*Coast Guard equivalent to "It's after five, time for a drink."*

THE FOLLOWING DAY Jackie kept her head buried in her work, managing to forget about Scott for large chunks of time, and then she'd hear a song playing from the bar down the street or catch a whiff of some delicious scent wafting from the food vendors along the beach and it would remind her of him.

Finally, she got up, shut the window, turned on the air-conditioning and went back to analyzing the data being sent to her computer through the satellite feed. She'd just shaken off lingering memories of last night in the aquarium when the doorbell rang.

Sighing, she put her laptop aside and got up. Who could it be? Not too many people knew she was here. She checked the peephole and when she saw Scott standing on the landing, her stomach took a nosedive at the same moment her heart soared. *Oh, stop it, seriously.*

It occurred to her that she did not have to answer the

door, but he rang again and a fluttery sensation went through her body.

His smile widened as if he knew she was watching him. In his hand he held a brown paper bag that he raised to the level of the peephole. On the paper bag were written the words in block letters: SCOTT'S HOME COOKING.

Don't answer it. Be strong.

She opened the door.

"Hey," he said, looking sheepish.

The old Jackie would have snapped his head off with a smart retort for interrupting her work, but this new sappy Jackie that she did not recognize stepped aside and let him in.

What the hell?

He held up one palm as if anticipating an argument. "I know you're busy and I don't want to interrupt your work, but I wanted to make sure you were eating right. You took care of me last night, I figured turnabout—"

That was as far as he got. She took the sack from his hand, set it on the table, then turned back to plant a big kiss on his lips.

"Wow," he said, "if this is what happens when a guy brings you food, I'm cooking for you all the time."

"Shh." She kissed him again, her fingers going to the buttons of his shirt.

It seemed her body had taken her mind hostage. She didn't think. Couldn't think. Not for one second. She just ripped his clothes off and it didn't take long before Scott was doing some equally enthusiastic ripping of his own.

In under a minute they were naked and Jackie was lying under him on the floor of her living room carpet. Both of them breathing like runners on the last mile of the Boston Marathon.

Their gazes meshed and they fell down the well of each other. Scott's masculine energy filled Jackie to the brim. There was no room for anything else but him. He stoked in her a desperate, insatiable thirst. A thirst so vast all the oceans of the world evaporated to a single drop.

How could this be? How could she have become so deliriously bewitched by him?

This bombardment of emotions terrified her.

The air between them vibrated. Each molecule alive with awareness. Their entire time together had been like this. A daring adventure.

At last, Jackie understood why she'd always been blasé about sex. No man had ever made her feel this way. Feminine. Wanted. Sexually powerful.

It felt glorious.

And scary as hell.

He was glorious. All biceps and triceps and gluts and hamstrings. She couldn't ever remember having such a well-built lover. She would remember this man's body for a long time to come.

And his face! Straight out of a daydream—square jaw, prominent cheekbones, dark hair.

She thought he was quivering, but then realized it was her, shaking so hard she couldn't catch her breath. Why was she trembling?

His hand was a silken glide, his lips delicious. He swirled his fingers over her navel. Softly and sweetly, he kissed the leaping pulse at her neck. He dropped down the length of her throat, and then took tiny succulent nibbles.

Then his tongue went traveling farther south, flicking out to lick one tight nipple, while his thumb achingly rubbed the other straining bud, drawing it into his furnace of a mouth. His thigh tightened against her leg and his abdominal muscles hardened to pure, smooth steel.

"Scott…" She breathed his name on a sigh.

Then he did something so wonderful with his illicit tongue that her eyes flew open and she lifted her head up off the floor. She had to see what he was doing to make her feel so good. Her gaze latched on his lips as she watched him drawing her nipple slowly in and out between his teeth.

She dropped her head to the ground, arched her back. "Go lower."

He dipped his head, trailing his tongue down the middle of her chest to the flat of her sternum before he veered off into other territory.

His hand danced at the juncture of her thighs. She parted her legs, allowing him to slip a finger between them.

And then his mouth and his fingers were in the same place. His lips closed around the tiny throbbing head of her cleft while his fingers tickled her entrance.

"Yes," she hissed as he moved his mouth back and forth, his silky hair a glossy glide between her fingers. "That's it."

She surfed the flow of emotions, navigating the swell of bliss and longing and discovery with unexpected dexterity. His warmth embraced her, bracing as a hug and she experienced a sense of rightness with him that she'd never felt before.

He took her up to a place she never knew existed. He was a fascinating adventure and she couldn't get enough.

A sudden bittersweet sensation seized her. This moment could not last. She knew that. She closed her eyes, determined to ignore the overwhelming sadness. It was okay. The feeling would pass. Honestly, this was all she needed from him. One brief slice of pleasure. Delicious and homey as apple pie with vanilla ice cream.

And he was licking at her as if she was indeed vanilla ice cream, sending sweet shock waves of sensation throughout her body. Binding her to him with wiredrawn skill.

She broke all at once. Fragile as the thinnest peanut brittle. The orgasm hit and she shattered, breaking into pieces in his strong, safe Coast Guard arms.

Ten minutes later, with his face buried against her neck, Scott murmured something.

"What?" Jackie whispered dreamily, her foggy gaze skimming the ceiling.

"I didn't come here for this," he said. "I promise."

"You're forgiven." She smiled.

He propped himself up on one elbow, peered down at her. "I came here to feed you."

"There's all kind of ways of feeding a woman," she observed.

"Are you hungry?"

"Ravenous."

Lazily, he crawled over to where she'd left the paper bag he'd brought and he carried it back to her. She propped herself up against the couch. Scott opened the sack, removed a Tupperware dish of chicken and dumplings and two spoons.

"You came prepared."

"Always ready," he quipped. "I'm Coast Guard." He spooned up a mouthful. "Have a bite."

She opened her mouth and he slipped the spoon between her parted teeth, feeding her. Then he took a bite for himself.

The delicious flavor of down-home comfort food delighted her taste buds. A bit of manna from heaven. And he'd made it for her from scratch.

"You're an excellent cook."

"Not really. My repertoire is pretty limited. Scrambled eggs, sandwiches, chicken and dumplings and key lime cheesecakes."

"Hey, you've got me. If it can't be microwaved, I'm lost."

It seemed incongruous to be eating dinner in the nude in the middle of the afternoon with her red-hot lover, but here she was.

Romantic. This is too damned romantic.

Yes, but she was hungry and the food was so good. Once they'd polished off the chicken and dumplings, they turned to his key lime cheesecake.

"Mmm." Jackie moaned. "I think that key lime cheesecake is going to bring me to a second orgasm."

Scott grinned. "Here. Let's push you over the edge. Have another bite."

"You're the devil, you know that?" she said and swallowed another mouthful of cheesecake.

You're getting in too deep. You gotta put a stop to this while you still can.

She knew it was true. Scott was making her feel things that threatened to upset everything she'd built. She handed him the container of cheesecake. "Thanks," she mumbled. "That's enough for me."

Quickly, her chest tightening with emotions she did not want to examine, Jackie got to her feet and began picking up her clothes. She couldn't believe how dumb she'd been about him.

"Jackie," he murmured.

"Uh-huh." She didn't look at him as she pulled on her cutoff blue jean shorts.

"You're running scared again."

"No." She shook her head. Denying it to both of them. "I just have work to do."

"There's nothing to be scared of."

That is where you are so wrong.

"Just talk to me. Tell me what you're feeling." He came to stand behind her. He was still naked, his clothes strewn over her apartment.

"You shouldn't have come here today," she whispered despondently. "I didn't want you to come here today."

"And yet, you let me in."

"It was a mistake."

He took hold of her shoulders, turned her around and forced her to look into his face. "Was it?"

She didn't want to hurt him, but she had to get rid of him. To protect herself. He had the potential to destroy her completely. "I told you from the beginning this could be nothing but casual sex."

"I told you I was fine with that."

Jackie drew in a shaky breath. "But here's the deal. I'm not."

"You're not?" His eyes lit up with the fire of hope and Jackie knew it was true. He did want more than a casual fling and she simply could not risk everything she'd ever worked for on the possibility of some unobtainable dream.

"But it doesn't matter what I want. You're not what I need, Scott Everly. You're a distraction and before this thing grows out of control, I think it's better if we cut all ties. I wish you a very happy life, but now it's time for you to leave."

TWO DAYS AFTER Jackie kicked him out of her apartment for bringing her food, Scott sat on a bar stool at the

Conch Café nursing a beer and thinking about Jackie. His ego stung. He thought they'd had fun. He'd had fun.

Face it. She's too busy for more than a quick roll around the aquarium. No muss. No fuss. Let it go.

Except, no matter how hard he tried he couldn't seem to turn loose the thought of her.

Yes, Scott's six-month-long dry spell was over. He should have been happy.

He was not.

For one thing, he could not get Jackie out of his senses. His fingertips had absorbed the memory of her skin. Whenever he rubbed them together, they still tingled with the feel of her.

He could smell her, too. Unique, surprising, womanly. The flavor of her lingered on his tongue—slightly tart, yet sweet, crisp and fresh as lemonade. Yes, her taste reminded him of fresh-squeezed lemonade. And there was the sound of her laughter. Soft and low and thoroughly original.

So what? She made it clear she didn't want anything more from you than sex. And here's the thing, buddy, is it really anything more than sex? You know how you get. Once you make love to a woman, it's like popcorn at the movies. You've got to have it. What's wrong with just sex?

Nothing.

There was nothing wrong with just sex, but he was starting to feel a lot more for her than that, and he wasn't ready to go there.

Good thing she put on the brakes. Excellent job, Jackie.

Scott took a sip of beer, stared brooding at the sun hovering on the horizon. Damn sunset. Why did it have to be so brutally romantic?

He was keeping his distance. Just like Jackie wanted.

Although every morning he kayaked past her research site in the mangrove channel hoping to find her there, but no dice. During the day, his mother and Megan kept him busy. Sending him on wedding-related errands. But in the evenings, he had nothing to do but think of Jackie.

Gorgeous Jackie Birchard.

"Want another beer?" Tad asked.

"I'm good."

"Just let me know when you want a refill."

"Will do." Scott nodded.

At the other end of the bar were some rowdy frat boys cutting up. They shoved each other and a beer bottle shattered against the tile floor.

"Your customers call." Scott inclined his head toward the drunken trio.

"Hey, hey," Tad yelled and snapped his fingers at the guys. "Support your local Coast Guard. Get lost."

"Huh?" It took the dense frat boys a few minutes to realize they were being thrown from the bar.

"Whaddya mean?" asked one of the frat boys.

"That's one broken beer bottle too many." Tad pointed toward the door.

"Says who?"

Scott tensed with interest. If Tad needed help, he'd be happy to help disperse those bozos. Maybe a good fist-fight was exactly what he needed to clear Jackie from his head.

"Never mind," mumbled the frat boy who'd broken the bottle. "Let's get out of this dump. Service sucked anyway."

To Scott's disappointment, they wandered off. Tad got a broom and dustbin from the back room and went past mumbling, "Tourists."

As the frat boys staggered out, a familiar face wandered in. Scott took another sip of beer as Carl Dugan in uniform took the empty seat next to him.

"Wanna beer? I'm buying."

"Let's get a table on the patio. It's more private," Carl suggested.

"Sure."

They found a table outside. Scott couldn't help noticing it was right next to the table he'd shared with Jackie. He shrugged off that thought and buttonholed a passing waitress to place an order for Carl's beer and an appetizer plate of soft-shell crabs.

"How's the investigation going?" Scott asked.

"Not great."

Ah, something interesting he could sink his teeth into. Something to do besides mooning over Jackie Birchard. This was exactly what he needed. Scott sat up straight. "What's up?"

"We arrested a young woman in the mangrove channel with five kilos of coke in her boat."

"That's great news!"

"Except that we have no way to tie her to DeCristo. She's refusing to talk. I'm more certain than ever that he's got stealth technology on a drone submarine, but I have absolutely no way of proving it."

Scott ran a hand over his jaw, gone scruffy with beard. He hadn't bothered shaving since the night Jackie told him to get lost. "There's gotta be a way to trap DeCristo."

"I'm open to suggestions." Carl spread his palms. "How do you catch a ghost? He uses mules and pawns and minions. Never gets his own hands dirty."

Good question.

"What about the tourist you arrested? The one who spilled his guts to cop a plea bargain? Do you think we could use him to set up some kind of sting operation?"

Carl tilted his head. "What do you have in mind?"

"Could you swing it with the D.A. to get the charges reduced if the guy agrees to help us nail DeCristo?"

"I'll look into it." Carl took a slug off his beer. "Let's say the tourist agrees to act in a sting and we get the D.A.'s backing. How would we swing this?"

"That would be the tricky part."

"You're telling me. DeCristo is slippery as an eel. I mean, c'mon. How did he get his hands on stealth technology? He's got friends in very high places and it's going to take a lot to lure him to the States. He's not stupid. He'll send henchmen."

"What's his biggest weakness?"

"Money?"

"Yeah, but go beyond that. What drives him?"

Carl gave it some thought. "Pride?"

"He's got an ego the size of South America."

"So how do we use that to our advantage?"

"That's something to ponder."

"We have to find a way to get our hands on that submarine. He thinks he's got us outfoxed."

"He does." Scott paused. "So far."

"Any thoughts on how we can get a bead on this invisible submarine?"

"He's got to have some kind of shipment schedule," Scott said. "Perhaps we can piece together the timing of his shipments between what your informant tells us and the behavior of the girl you arrested. Even if she won't talk, her actions speak volumes. We can track her movements over the last few months, see if we can uncover a pattern. I bet we can paint a picture of when and where the deliveries are occurring. Here's a thought. What if instead of the tourist to spring the trap we convince the D.A. to let the girl go so we can track her."

"I wish I could," Carl said. "But I don't have the man-power for that."

Scott held his arms wide. "What am I? Chopped liver?"

"Megan's wedding is on Saturday."

"I've got Wednesday and Thursday to get started."

Carl pondered this. "Okay. Speak to the D.A. and see what you can arrange."

Scott rubbed his palms together. "I can't wait to get to work."

And to fill my head with something besides Jackie Birchard.

11

Support your local Coast Guard…get lost.
        —Tad Winston, bartender at the Conch Café
                            and Coast Guard wannabe

JACKIE MADE GOOD USE of her Scott-less time. She wrote
fifty pages on her dissertation. Spent hours at the library.
Checked on her monitoring equipment in the mangrove
channel twice a day. Each time making sure to go at
noon, in spite of the sultry heat because she knew Scott
kayaked the mangrove channel in the morning and she
didn't want to risk running into him.

Things were cruising splendidly. She made up for the
time she wasted hanging out with him. Especially because she was having trouble sleeping. When she lay in
bed, all she saw was Scott's face. She tasted his kisses.
Felt his body moving inside hers. Her treacherous libido
whispered, asking her to phone him for a booty call, but
she didn't want to stir things up again. This would pass.
All she had to do was wait it out.

On Wednesday, she padded to the refrigerator to get
something to eat for lunch. Scott had rubbed off on
her and she realized he was right. If she didn't eat on

a regular schedule she couldn't stay healthy enough to do her work.

But there was nothing in her fridge except a bottle of ketchup, a pint of milk on the verge of going bad and a stick of butter. The pantry was equally bare. She'd polished off the last of her corn flakes that morning. She was going to have to make a trip to the market.

It'll do you good to get out of the house. You've been holed up for days.

Yes, it would do her good, but she hated shopping. Sighing, she slipped on flip-flops, grabbed her house keys and walked to the convenience store at the end of the block.

Once she was outside, she saw there was some kind of street festival going on. Tourists in Hawaii shirts, fanny packs and sandals thronged the sidewalks. The street had been blocked off with sawhorse barricades. Kiosks had been set up, selling everything from seashells to seascape art to birdhouses, wind chimes and whimsical yard flags.

Food carts sprawled lazily in the mix. The smell of sizzling fajitas mingled with the fragrance of hot dogs and funnel cakes. Kids licked ice-cream cones or frozen limeades. Parents carried beer, wine, iced tea and sodas.

The convenience seemed suddenly miles away. Jackie decided to grab a turkey leg and head back to the apartment. She could go shopping when the street festival was over.

She moved to queue up at a kiosk selling roast turkey legs and chicken satay and steak on a stick when she heard a familiar laugh. A thrill of excitement ran up her back, immediately followed by panic. She'd know that laugh anywhere.

Scott.

An instant smile hit her lips before she could stop it

and she turned toward the sound of his laugh like a sunflower soaking up sunbeams.

She spied him over by a jewelry kiosk flirting with a red-haired woman in a purple dress and wide-brimmed straw hat. The woman was gazing at him as if she'd just found a gold Krugerrand lying on the street. She chuckled silkily and leaned against him as if they were together.

Jackie gulped. Felt her pulse stutter, sputter, stumble.

Scott was with another woman. A younger, prettier woman.

Don't tell me you're jealous. Good grief, Jackie, you do not get jealous over guys. You don't have a jealous bone in your body.

Except right now she was so jealous she was certain her eyes had turned green.

You're the one who told him it was over. Well, looks like he took you at your word.

"What'll you have?" the man behind the counter asked.

Jackie blinked. "Huh?"

"Turkey leg, chicken satay, steak on a stick?"

"Nothing," she said, suddenly not the least bit hungry. She got out of line.

Heat from the cement radiated up through her thin flip-flops. She spun around quickly, praying that Scott hadn't seen her, and she rushed back to her apartment as fast as she could push through the crowd.

"So, WHAT DO YOU DO for a living?" Scott asked the redhead that Carl had busted with cocaine. He'd called the D.A. on Tuesday night and convinced him the woman was integral to getting a lead on DeCristo. A deal had been struck and the redhead released on bail this morning. Her name was Juliette Sterns. She was from Miami, a model, and apparently had developed quite a taste for the white powder.

Scott had been at the courthouse when they let her out that morning, pretending he'd just been released on bail, as well. He chatted her up, and asked her to the street festival. He'd flashed a big grin and she'd said yes without hesitation.

He was a flirt. Always had been, but he was finding it damn hard to be civil to DeCristo's little drug mule. His father's face kept flashing into his mind.

Steady. Keep up the charade. Finally you have a chance to avenge his death. Don't blow it.

A smile tipped her lips. "Oh, this and that."

"Doesn't sound like it pays the bills."

"Oh." She fluttered her eyelashes. "You'd be surprised."

He had to glance away to keep distaste from showing on his face. That was when he saw Jackie.

She was walking away from him as fast as her legs would carry her, but he'd know that sway, those cutoff blue jeans anywhere. Had she seen him flirting with the redhead? Was that why she was running away?

You wish she was jealous. Face it. Jackie is not as into you as you're into her.

"Listen," Scott said, giving his attention back to the redhead, even though his gut tugged at him to go check on Jackie. "I'd like to get to know you better. Can I take you to dinner tonight."

"Nooo, not tonight," she said. "I have to work."

His ears pricked up. Could she possibly be picking up another shipment from DeCristo tonight? "Doing this and that?"

"You've got it."

"That's a shame. I really wanted to see you."

"You can take me somewhere right now," she enticed. "I'm hungry, you're hungry. We're here together."

Dammit, if he was going to do this, he needed to fully have his head in the game, not pine over Jackie.

Do your job, Everly.

"Sure," he said, "why not now. You like shrimp?"

"Love it."

"I know the perfect place. Follow me." Then with that, he let Jackie go and focused on his task, just as he always did.

Later. He would go to Jackie later.

JACKIE SHOULDN'T HAVE looked back, but she had to know. Was Scott really with that other woman or had he merely been talking to her?

Why do you care? Forget him.

But her body couldn't forget. She yearned to be joined with him again.

And again and again and again.

All the more reason to forget him.

She dodged behind a family of tourists and peered around to see if she could spot Scott. Yes. There he was. With his hand to the redhead's back, guiding her toward his rental car.

All the air leaked from her body. Well, that was that.

Let it go. Let him go.

Good advice. Could she heed it?

Determined, Jackie turned and ran smack-dab into Megan Everly. "Oh!" she exclaimed as Megan put up a hand.

"Whoa, Jackie, where's the fire?"

Jackie plastered a smile on her face. "Hi."

"I thought that was you, so I came over to say hello."

"Yep, it's me."

Megan wore a tie-dyed sundress and espadrilles. "I didn't get to tell you goodbye the other night."

"I'm sorry for running out on your—"

"No need to explain." Megan gave her a knowing wink. "I saw the way you and my brother were looking at each other and I just have to tell you how pleased I am that you two have found each other and—"

"I'm afraid you've gotten the wrong idea about Scott and me. We're not a couple."

"I get it." Megan nodded. "It's still too new and you don't want to jinx things by talking about it. I completely understand. Dave and I went out for three months before I was brave enough to tell my mom that I'd found someone special. Love is scary stuff."

Love? Megan was so off base. She wasn't in love with Scott.

"Your brother and I are just..." What was she going to say? Sex buddies? Thank God, she'd held her tongue for once instead of blurting out the truth. "Having fun," she finished.

"That's what Dave and I told ourselves in the beginning and look at us now." Megan flashed her two-karat diamond engagement ring. "Getting married on Saturday."

"I know you two are going to be so happy." Nervously, Jackie shifted her weight from foot to foot.

"Listen." Megan rested a hand on Jackie's shoulder. "I meant to ask you this the other night but things got really busy and we didn't get a chance to talk again, but you are invited to the wedding. I told Scott to ask you, but I know he's probably thinking your relationship is too new for a wedding, and if you feel the same way, I understand, but I would really love it if you could come. You mean a lot to Scott, and Scott means a lot to me."

Jackie thought about the redhead. That showed how well Megan knew her brother. Not well at all. He'd already moved on. "I do appreciate the invitation, but I've got a lot of work to do on my dissertation—"

Megan's smile faltered, but she quickly caught it and lifted her lips brightly. "Yes, well, I just wanted to put that out there. Just in case you were interested. I like you, Jackie."

Jackie had very few female friends. Hell, who was she kidding? She had very few friends of either sex. She was so into her work that she rarely took time to develop relationships beyond acquaintances and she wasn't going to do it now. "Um, I like you, too, Megan."

And she did, but she doubted they had anything in common. Megan was one of those perky bright-eyed glass-half-full kind of girls. The kind who made great wives and mothers. The kind Jackie had never been nor understood.

A shadow of loneliness passed over her. What would it feel like to be normal? To love clothes and food and shopping? To put a high premium on female friendships?

"I hope to see you at the wedding." She touched Jackie's arm and then she gave her a little wave and headed off into the crowd.

Well, that served only to send her even further down into the dumps. First seeing Scott with another woman. Then bumping into sweet Megan, who reminded her of all the things she would never be. Jackie trudged back to her apartment, feeling lower than she'd felt in a very long time.

SCOTT'S LUNCH DATE with Juliette Sterns turned out to be a bust. She talked constantly of some reality television show about modeling and how she hoped to try out for it. That was until he finally asked her if she liked to party.

Her eyes glimmered. "What you do mean by party?"

"You know what I mean." He reached across the table and rubbed his thumb over her knuckles when what he wanted to do was grab her, shake her silly and demand she tell him what the hell she was doing working for a scumbag like DeCristo.

"You mean more than alcohol, right?" Her eyes narrowed in a wicked expression.

He arched an eyebrow.

"Do you enjoy cola?"

He realized it was code for cocaine. "Yes. Do you know where I can get some?"

She nodded. "Premium product."

Scott sat up straight. "I'm interested."

"It doesn't come cheap."

"'Course not."

She named a price that had him pressing his lips together to keep from whistling.

"It's worth it," she promised.

"When can I get some?" he asked, wondering how he was going to turn this conversation to her supplier.

"It's not quite that simple," she said. "Since I got pinched by the cops I'm not in a position to pick it up and because of that, there's a freeze from the supply end."

"When do you anticipate a thaw?"

"Maybe in a few days, but I can't be the one to intercept, if you follow me."

"You need someone to be your bag boy."

She pointed a finger at him. "You're sharp."

He shook his head. "You know, I don't do business

with people I don't know. If I'm going to help you out, I need to meet your supplier."

"No, no." She shook her head vigorously. "That's not possible."

Don't press. Don't scare her off.

He shrugged. "Too bad."

She studied him a long moment. "I wish I could make introductions but the supplier never comes to the U.S. I've never dealt with him directly."

"That's fine. Say no more. You ready to go?" Scott pulled out his wallet, laid thirty dollars on the table to cover their lunch and the tip.

"I could maybe introduce you to one of his associates here in the Keys."

It was a start. Should he take it?

"Sorry," he said smoothly, even as he worried that he was making a grave mistake. "Got a pen?"

"Oh, sure." She dug a pen from her purse and passed it to him.

He wrote his cell phone number down on a napkin. "Here's my number. Call me if things change."

"Thanks." She folded the napkin, put it in her purse. "Um…I had a nice time."

"Me, too," he lied.

"Do you think we could see each other again?"

He wrinkled his nose. "Come through for me on the cola and we'll see."

Then with that, he turned and walked away. Hopefully, that would give the redhead something to think about.

JACKIE WASN'T SURE WHY she went to Megan's wedding. Perhaps it was because the four walls of her apartment were closing in. Maybe it was because her search for the

Key blenny had stalled, her theory going nowhere. Or maybe, just maybe, she missed Scott so much she had to see him again.

Plus, she was terrified he'd taken her advice and already moved on with the redhead.

He did what you told him to. You have no right to take him to task.

Jackie walked into the botanical garden where the ceremony was being held. She felt awkward and out of place in the same dress she'd worn to Megan's party the previous weekend. It wasn't right that she'd worn white today. Only the bride should wear white on her wedding day, right?

Oh, crap. This was embarrassing. She knew nothing about these social rules. Maybe she could just slip out before anyone saw her.

"Jackie!" Scott's mother spied her, broke away from the group of people she was speaking with and came across the lawn toward her. "You made it. Megan is going to be so happy to see you."

"Thank you all for inviting me."

"But of course." Shannon Everly beamed. "Any friend of Scott's is a friend of the entire family."

Even the redhead?

"I brought a gift." Jackie held out the wedding present. It was a silver picture frame.

"What a lovely gesture. Let me show you where you can put it." Shannon led her to a table overflowing with gifts.

Jackie settled her gift on the table with the others.

"Well, well, if it isn't the mangrove mermaid."

At the sound of Scott's voice, Jackie's stomach dipped to her shoes. What was this power he held over her? All she had to do was hear his voice and her knees went to rubber.

She turned to find Shannon drifting off with a dreamy smile on her face and Scott standing in front of her looking like a complete daydream in a tuxedo, a gardenia boutonniere at his lapel.

His eyes held a soft warmth. "I'm glad you came."

Jackie shrugged. "Megan invited me."

"She'll be happy you showed. I'm happy you showed."

"Are you really?"

"I am." He sounded completely sincere.

They stood looking at each other. Finally, unable to stand the tension, Jackie dropped her gaze.

"I have to go do my brotherly duty and walk my sister down the aisle in place of my father, but let me escort you to your seat."

"Thank you."

Scott took her arm and tucked it through his. It felt so good being this close to him.

That was the problem. It felt too good.

He guided her to a folding chair adorned with a white slipcover. He leaned over and whispered, "You look gorgeous." Then he winked and disappeared.

"Aren't you a lucky one," said the elderly woman sitting beside her.

"Excuse me?"

"That Scottie, he's a hottie. Half the women in Key West are in love with him. Me included. They're going to be so disappointed to hear he's finally gotten serious about someone."

"Oh, no." Jackie shook her head. "We're not serious."

"That's what you think."

"What does that mean?" Jackie asked, a fresh round of thrill-fear shooting through her.

The music started and the elderly lady placed an index finger over her mouth. "Shh."

Okay, shut up. Let the wedding begin.

The ceremony lasted forty minutes and was one of the most beautiful weddings she'd ever been to. Granted, she'd only been to two other weddings, but still. The garden setting was soothing. Puffy white clouds floated overhead. The air smelled of fresh-mown grass, gardenia and citronella. Megan's bridal gown was simple and elegant. A delirious smile graced the groom's face.

Scott gave Megan away, then sat down in the front row beside his mother. Jackie studied the back of his head, admiring his thick dark hair cut close, but not too short. He had a strong neck. Tanned and muscular but not bullish. His ears did not stick out the way some men's did.

He was so perfect.

Her breath slipped quickly between her parted teeth. *He can't be perfect. The perfect guy for you is another scientist who will be as lost in his work as you are in yours. He's got flaws. Everyone had flaws. He could be nosy and he liked helping people far too much.* What was that about? He was too heroic for her. She had a cranky side. A self-absorbed side. She couldn't be right for a man who loved the world in an open-arms embrace.

Regret flitted through her and she hovered on the verge of tears.

What was this? Jackie Birchard was not emotional. She very rarely cried. She was tough and dedicated and going gooey as ice cream in the sun as Megan and Dave exchanged vows.

Hormones. PMS. The wedding ceremony. All of it? Who knew?

Stop it. Just sit here until it's over and then you can slip out.

Except that wasn't the way things turned out. The minute Dave and Megan raced grinning up the aisle, Scott got to his feet and came over to her, moving before the rest of the crowd had a chance to get on their feet.

"We've got to go take pictures," he said, "but don't you dare go away."

"Okay," she agreed and stayed put.

Later, at the start of the reception, Scott reappeared. "You're sitting beside me."

"No, no." She shied. "I can't sit up front with the wedding party."

"Says who?"

"Emily Post."

Scott laughed. "Don't try to convince me that you know the first thing about wedding protocol, Jackie Birchard. You couldn't give two hoots in the wind about it."

"You got me."

"So come on."

"I don't know much but I'm sure it's a faux pas."

"I have Megan's blessing. Dave's, too."

"I can't."

"You have to work."

"Well, yes, but that's not all. If I sit with you, what will people think?"

"That you're with me."

"Exactly."

His smile disappeared. "Is being with me such a bad thing?"

"I can't promise anything, Scott."

"I'm not asking for any promises, Jackie. All you have to do is sit there and eat. No obligations."

"You're sure?"

"Cross my heart."

"Fine," she agreed warily.

It turned out to be fine. The food was delicious, the toasts hilarious. Scott substituted for his father and danced with Megan for the father-daughter dance. Then afterward he handed his sister off to Dave, and went back for Jackie.

She hung back. "I don't dance."

"Today you do. This is once and for all your last chance for a first dance. It's happening tonight."

Part of her wanted to dance. In fact, she was tapping her toes in time to the music, but part of her was afraid of looking like a clumsy fool.

"I'll take care of everything," Scott said. "Just trust me."

Ah, that was the heart of it. Jackie had trouble trusting anyone to have her back. She'd been disappointed numerous times by the people in her life who were supposed to have her back. Her mother. Her father. Jed. Trusting Scott was a huge leap of faith.

But he was smiling and holding out his hand and in that moment Jackie felt another brick fall from the castle wall she'd built around her heart.

"Trust me, Jackie."

Resisting Scott was like trying to stand upright in a level-five hurricane on the deck of a lurching merchant ship. She took his hand and the smile that reached his eyes almost broke her heart. He looked so honest, so genuine, so happy to be here with her. She didn't deserve someone as real as him. "Scott—"

"Jackie." He pulled her to him and propelled her onto the dance floor.

They swayed underneath the white canopy. Cream-colored candles flickered from the luminaries on the tables. Dancing couples surrounded them but it seemed as if they were all alone on their own little island. She clung to Scott like a life raft.

Jackie took a deep breath and leaned her head against his shoulder, allowing herself to be swept away. She hugged the moment. Hugged this memory close to her heart. She would treasure this first dance forever.

He rested his cheek against her head and they moved in tempo to the song. It was as if the band had tailored the tune to fit Jackie and Scott.

Jackie took a deep breath and resolved to be happy for now. Whatever happened after this did not matter. All that mattered was this moment. With the Japanese lanterns strung overhead lighting up the sky as day drifted into night.

They danced four more songs without sitting down. She knew Scott was in good shape, but she was stunned by his stamina. "How is your leg?" she asked.

"What leg?"

"Shark bite all healed?"

"Good enough. It's not slowing me down."

"Nothing slows you down."

"Except speed bump Jackie."

"Well, you did have me spinning my wheels for a while." She tilted her head.

"My place isn't far from here."

"Are you suggesting what I think you're suggesting?" She smiled impishly.

"I hope so."

"Are we making up?" she asked.

"I want to."

"We are," she confirmed, even as a small part of her whispered, *You're going to get your first broken heart, Jackie Birchard. Just you wait and see.*

12

Now stand by for heavy rolls as the ship comes about.

*—Coast Guard quote on a wall plaque
in Scott's vacation bungalow*

SCOTT TOOK HER BACK to his bungalow. His heart thumped with happiness to have Jackie with him again.

When Megan told him that she'd invited Jackie to the wedding, he'd been jacked up on hope. He'd cleaned the bungalow and stocked up on condoms. He was Coast Guard, after all. *Semper Paratus.* Always prepared.

She stood in the middle of the living room, hands clasped behind her back, studying the paneled wall. Her gaze traveled over a hand-carved plaque. "Now stand by for heavy rolls as the ship comes about." She flicked a gaze at him. "What does that mean?"

"Roll with the punches, because they are going to come."

"Interesting." Her gaze shifted to the seascape paintings. "These are beautiful. Who painted them?"

"My father," Scott said. "It was his hobby."

"How did he die?"

"Line of duty," Scott said, tight-lipped.

"You must really be missing him today," she said, and he was surprised to see a fine mist of tears gleaming in her eyes.

"Yeah," he admitted.

"You need a distraction." Her hand went to the button of her dress. He loved the way the hem floated around her slender, tanned legs.

"It wouldn't hurt."

"I can be that for you."

He went to her then, stripping off the bow tie of his tuxedo as he walked. "Jackie," he whispered.

She twined her arms around his neck, tugged his hand down to her sweet, honeyed lips.

And all the pain and sorrow and loneliness he would have been feeling over his father's absence vanished in the power of her kiss.

They kissed for a long time, slowly undressing each other, garment by garment. Off came his jacket. Her necklace vanished. She removed his cummerbund. He dismantled her dress. Her fingers worked the buttons of his white shirt, one by one. His hand unsnapped her bra.

Finally, they were both naked in front of each other, the moonlight spilling through the open blinds, bathing them in moon glow. The smell of gardenias was everywhere.

He kissed her again. Her eyelids, her nose, her chin, her cheeks. He wanted this to be the opposite of their fevered joining in the aquarium and at her apartment. He wanted to *make love* all night long.

He bent at the waist, swept her off her feet and carried her into his bedroom. He draped her across his bed and then stepped back to look at her. To savor this moment. In his eyes, she'd never looked more beautiful. Vulnerable, but at last willing to take a chance on something more than casual sex.

"You are amazing," he murmured.

"You're not so bad yourself, Coast Guard. Now bring that jackhammer over here and nail me."

He laughed. He had to admire her forthrightness. Jackie was not a woman who beat around the bush. He sank down on the bed beside her, peered into her eyes. "Remember the night I chased you?"

"How could I forget? It was the most scared I'd ever been."

"I didn't mean to alarm you."

"You want to know what really scared me?" she whispered, not shying from the intensity of his gaze. Scott considered that a triumph. That she was able to be honest with him.

"I do."

"I sort of liked it."

"The chase?"

"The danger."

"Hmm, have you ever thought about joining the Coast Guard? We could use someone with your diving skills."

She laughed and traced a finger over his chest. "I'd settle for just joining with this Coast Guard."

"Well, why didn't you just say so." He gathered her to him, amazed at how strong and secure he felt with her in his arms.

Her fingers tracked from his chest to the puckered scar on the inside of his right upper arm. "How'd you get this?"

"My first time at sea as an officer. We were engaged in a drug interdiction between California and Mexico. The smugglers tried to outrun us, but we had a brand-new state-of-the-art cutter. As a last gasp, they started shooting at us with harpoon guns."

"Heavy duty."

"Harpoon went halfway through my arm. Lucky for me, it missed bone."

She kissed his wound. "I'm sorry you got hurt."

"I'm Coast Guard. I wouldn't have it any other way. It's part of the job."

"I see."

"Does that scare you?"

"Why would it scare me? It's who you are."

"Jackie," he murmured, "where have you been all my life?"

They kissed some more, slowly exploring each other from their lips on down. He paid a lot of attention to her breasts, learning what made her shake her head, what caused her to make soft keening noises and pull in air through clenched teeth.

"That's it, mermaid. Let me know what you want."

But Jackie wasn't selfish. She gave as good as she got. Her mouth was as adventuresome as his, seeking, tasting, on a search-and-find mission that left Scott with his eyes rolling back in his head as her daring little tongue explored the hardest part of him.

The minute her lips were around his shaft, he felt his world shatter into pure, blue-ribbon pleasure. Some women didn't enjoy doing this, but Jackie...well, Jackie took him with gusto. And when he quickly exploded, she swallowed him up, smiling wide and batting her lashes.

He collapsed into the mattress, his fingers fisted around the pillow he pulled over his face, drained, but not sated.

Oh, no, this was only the beginning. As soon as he recovered from the earth-moving blow job she'd given him, he turned the tables, anchoring her spread-eagle to the bed with his silk ties. He went down on her and she went wild. Calling him all kinds of names, both exalting and cursing him as he teased and tempted, dragged things out and made her beg.

"You're wicked," she gasped.

"No more so than you."

She tasted gloriously good. She was soft and warm and wet and damn, he couldn't get enough of her. His tongue plied her and she responded to each lick, caress, touch. The woman who lived in her mind and kept her heart locked up had an incredibly responsive body.

"I'm gonna take you down, babe."

"Promises, promises."

"Oh, don't taunt me. You're in for it."

"Prove it."

"Saucy. You wanna live on the edge?"

"Yes. Give me all you've got."

He did. Sucking her sweet clit until she screamed his name over and over and over again.

Feeling very proud of himself, he untied her and held her gently as she shivered in his arms. He kissed her temple and smoothed her hair and wondered if he'd died and gone to heaven.

"Now," she said, "my turn to be in charge."

He had no problem with that. He rolled over onto his back, his prick miraculously hard again.

She straddled him and, giggling, stared down into his eyes; her blond hair fell over her cheeks, tumbled across his chest. His erection pulsed against her bottom. She leaned down to capture his mouth, her hair falling around them both like a silk curtain. He felt her warm, moist heat against his belly. When she had him writhing with need, she pulled back. "Condom?"

"Bedside drawer."

She reached over, dug one out, ripped open the package with her teeth and rolled it onto his very horny Johnson. Then, just to be sassy, she cupped his balls in her hands and applied gentle pressure while she took one of his nipples into her mouth.

"Whoa! You keep that up and I'll explode before you ever climb on board."

"Can't have that, can we?" She glanced up from his nipple and winked.

He wrapped his arms around her waist and guided her back into the straddle. She was on her knees, poised over him, his erection jumping and bobbing, waiting for her ultimate juiciness. "C'mon, put me out of my misery."

"I remember you were a bit relentless when I begged the same thing."

"I was so cruel."

"You were." She laughed.

"But you're not as mean as me."

"Don't be so sure about that." She started to ease down on him, but then at the last moment pulled up and out of reach.

Scott groaned. "Evil."

"Uh-huh."

"You like torturing me."

"Only in the best possible way."

"Cruel to be kind, eh?"

"You know it."

Then she slid down on him, taking the length of his erection in her, pressing her bottom fully against his pelvis.

"Jac-*kie*," he exclaimed as her muscles clamped around him.

"Scott-*y*," she gloated gleefully and began rocking into him hard.

Scott couldn't get enough of watching her. As his cock engorged fully and completely, his gaze traveled over her beautiful body. He was a lucky, lucky man. How had he gotten so lucky?

He reached up to capture her nipples between his thumbs and index fingers and soon her soft moans were in sync with his. *Yeah, baby, rock my world.*

She rode him hard. His hips bucking and thrusting, he tried to find some way of getting deeper inside her. She moved up and he felt bereft. Then she came down hard and he experienced rapture. Up and down. Despair, then joy. Frustration, then frenzy.

Then in one hot, fierce second, they came together. He exploded with a force he never believed possible, his climax shooting out hot and milky.

He felt her orgasm ripple over him in undulating waves, contracting and releasing up and down the length of his cock.

Glory. Pure glory.

He'd struck gold with her. He'd dated a lot of women, but none, not a single one, had ever made him feel as if he'd landed on the moon. He was an astronaut. Exploring an unknown landscape. There were no words for sex this good.

There was only the minnow of fear that something this red-hot was destined to burn out as quickly as it had rocketed him to the stars.

JACKIE AWOKE FEELING changed in a fundamental way.

She'd opened herself up to Scott in a way she'd never opened herself up to anyone before him. Not just her body, but her mind and her—dare she say it—heart, as well.

Because after they made love, they'd talked for hours. He told her about his dad. She found herself opening up and telling him that when her mother had left her father, she'd left Jackie, as well.

They commiserated on what it was like to lose a parent. Like it or not, it affected you, carved you into the person you became.

Scott told her about Amber, his one serious relationship. Since Jackie had never had what she considered a serious relationship, she mentioned only Boone and her regret that she'd never bothered really getting to know her half brother.

Then, far into the wee hours of the morning, they talked about their work and how much they both loved what they did for a living. After that, they made love again and fell asleep in each other's arms as the sunrise pushed up the shade of night.

She yawned, stretched, reached across the bed for Scott and her hand fell on an empty spot. Sitting up, she pushed a hank of hair from eyes and looked around the room.

The closet door hung open and his Coast Guard uniform dangled from a hanger. On the bedside table sat a book. The title made her smile. Rachel Carson's *Silent Spring.*

She cocked her head, listening for him, wondering if he was in the bathroom, but then her nose caught the scent of coffee, bacon and eggs. She threw back the covers. Where was her dress? She couldn't find it. Where had he taken if off her? Last night was such a delicious mishmash of memories, she couldn't remember. She padded to the bathroom and took a shower. She found a blue terry cloth bathrobe hanging on the back of the door, put it on and wandered into the kitchen.

"Morning, sleepyhead," Scott greeted her from his place at the stove. He was dressed in a pair of swim trunks and a Coast Guard T-shirt.

"You're making me breakfast?" She felt pleased and a sly voice in the back of her head whispered, *what if you could wake up to this every morning?*

"Sit," he said and served up a plate of scrambled eggs, bacon, toast and a cup of strong coffee. "Eat."

"You, too." She pointed at the chair beside her with the tines of her fork.

"Just dishing up my food now." He turned back to the stove, and then came to the table with a plate of his own.

"What time is it?" she asked.

"Ten o'clock."

She groaned. "I haven't slept this late since my under-grad days."

"Me, either." He grinned.

She giggled. "It feels decadent."

"Hey, it's important to break with routine now and again. Makes you feel free."

They were halfway through their intimate breakfast, stopping between bites to lean across the table to steal kisses, when Scott's cell phone rang.

He reached across to pluck it from the middle of the table, but not before Jackie saw a photo flash on the caller ID monitor. It was the redhead that she'd seen him with at the festival.

Jackie's stomach churned. Apparently, he liked the redhead well enough to program her picture into his phone.

She struggled not to feel anything, but she couldn't stop a wedge of jealousy from lodging in her throat, sharp as a cracker. She ducked her head, tried to fork another bite into her mouth, but she couldn't make herself swallow. Nor could she just spit it out.

So she sat there, scrambled eggs that seconds before had tasted delicious, now congealing into a cold mass on her tongue.

Scott pushed back his chair. "Please excuse me. I've gotta take this."

Jackie nodded. The egg seemed to expand, filling her entire mouth.

Scott got up, walked out on the porch. Clearly, he didn't want her overhearing his conversation.

The minute the door closed behind him, Jackie got up and spit the egg into the trash can. Dread had her pulling a hand over her mouth. She closed her eyes. The kitchen window was open. It looked out over the porch. Scott's conversation carried right into the kitchen along with the sea breeze.

"Sure, I can be there. Just tell me when and where," he purred to the redhead.

Disappointment knocked against Jackie's rib cage. Okay, she was lying to herself. It was more than just disappointment. She felt...*devastated.* Scott had just spent the night with her, bonded with her, and now he was making a date with another woman.

You were the one who told him you didn't want to be exclusive. What are you upset about?

What was she upset about?

Jackie paced the kitchen. She thought...she thought... oh, what in the hell had she thought? That this could have a fairy-tale happy ending? How stupidly ridiculous was that? She'd never been a happily-ever-after gal before. Why now did she suddenly want it?

Scott stepped back inside whistling the song they'd

danced to the night before—"Love Is an Ocean Wide."

"Hey." He stopped, studied her. "What's wrong?"

"Nothing." Jackie forced a smile.

"Don't lie to me, Jackie Birchard. I see right through you."

"Fine, okay, you want to know what's bothering me?"

"I do." He nodded.

"I know about her."

"About who?"

"Don't lie to *me*. I saw you with the redhead and now when she calls you take it out on the porch."

"That bothers you?" He looked amused at her jealousy. Amused! He was amused.

"Yes." She folded her arms over her chest. "I know it shouldn't bother me. It's stupid, but it does."

"You told me we couldn't have anything more than a casual fling."

"I know what I said."

"It's hypocritical of you to get jealous."

She sank her top teeth into her bottom lip. "I know. But don't go see her."

"I have to, Jackie."

"Why?"

"Things are complicated and for now I can't tell you about it, but listen to me when I tell you that this other woman means nothing to me."

"Then don't go see her."

"I don't have a choice."

"Then she must mean *something* to you."

"She does, but not in the way you think."

"So just tell me."

"I can't," he reiterated. "It's Coast Guard business. You just have to trust me on that."

Trust.

It was not something that came easily to her. She wanted to trust him, but she could not ignore the deep hurting in her heart. Oh, dear God, this was exactly what she'd wanted to avoid, feeling like this. Raw. Split in two.

She spied her dress lying in the living room. She bent to snatch it up. "I'm going to make this easy for you. Go to her. Don't worry about me. I've got my work…you've got yours. That's all we need. Right?"

"Wrong." His hand snaked out and snared her wrist.

Her temper flared. "Please let me go."

"Not until you listen to me."

Jackie glanced away.

Scott reached out, took her chin, forced her to meet his gaze. "We can sort this out, Jackie, just not right now. All I'm asking is that you trust me."

She jerked away. "I'm afraid I can't do that."

"Why not?"

Because she was scared out of her wits that he was lying. She was scared of what she was feeling. It was too much. Too powerful. It was better to cut her losses now and get out while the getting was good before she got her heart completely broken.

Too late, too late.

"Listen," she said. "I'm not angry. This is completely for the best. We had a great time." She waved a hand. "It was a lovely evening. Great. Beautiful. You're a good guy. I wish for you a very happy life."

"Seriously? You're breaking up with me again just because another woman called me?"

"Yes. No. It's not just that."

"What else is wrong?"

She shrugged. "Things are getting too complicated. I don't do complicated."

"Yes, yes, they are. But that's because you're feeling something for me."

"Things that I don't want to feel."

"Why not?"

"Because feelings are messy. They can get you hurt. Better to make a clean break of it now while we still can." Her chest heaved with the effort of breathing.

"Is that what you really want?" Sadness filled his eyes.

"It is."

He hardened his chin, stepped away from her. "Okay, fine. I've done my best to convince you that things could be great between us if you didn't keep putting up walls, but apparently you like life all by yourself under the sea, mermaid. You're free to go, but first, I want you to promise me one thing."

"What's that?" she asked begrudgingly.

"Stay out of the mangrove channel for the next few days."

"I will not. If I need to go—"

"Jackie!" he commanded, and stepped forward so suddenly that Jackie took an involuntary step back. "I'm not playing games here. This is the Coast Guard talking, not your midnight lover. Do not go into the mangrove channel until I call and tell you that's it's safe. Do I make myself perfectly clear?"

IT TOOK EVERY BIT of Coast Guard fortitude that Scott possessed not to tell her the truth about Juliette Sterns.

He hated to hurt her feelings. Hated seeing her in pain. It tore him up inside. But this was the way it had to be if he hoped to bring DeCristo to justice.

When this was over, he'd find a hundred ways to make it up to her. In the meantime, he had a lot of work to do.

Juliette had told him that a new shipment of drugs was arriving the following evening.

He called his boss in D.C., told him what was going on down here in the Keys. His boss green-lighted additional funds for interdiction to destroy DeCristo's operation.

Then Scott called Carl and told him what Juliette had told him. She would be picking up a delivery the next day in the mangrove channel and if he wanted a slice of the pie, he needed to bring her some money today.

After meeting with the D.A. on Monday morning, Scott met Juliette at the restaurant where they'd previously had lunch. He passed her fifty thousand dollars of marked government bills. They arranged a meeting time for later that evening for delivery of the product.

In the meantime, Carl got Coast Guard officers in place, hiding on the banks of the mangrove channel to intercept the transaction and take possession of DeCristo's drone submarine. They also put an undercover Coast Guard on Juliette and at sunset, Scott went to join Carl's crew in the mangrove channel.

All during the stakeout, Scott thought of Jackie. He couldn't shake her from his head. He should have his mind on capturing DeCristo's sub, but all he could do was think about how crushed Jackie had looked at the thought he was dating another woman. Hell, who would ever want another woman if they had Jackie?

Jackie.

She intrigued him like no woman ever had. Could he be falling in love?

It was a startling realization. He hadn't expected it, but she'd come blowing into his life like a hurricane. He had no gauge for what he was feeling. He only knew he couldn't imagine his life without her in it. He'd straighten this all out. One way or another he'd convince her they had something special.

The Coast Guard agents watched the mangrove channel for hours, but Juliette never showed up. What if Carl's tourist was wrong and DeCristo did not have a stealth submarine? What if it was all rumor and legend?

Scott's stomach soured that he'd pulled the brass in on the sting without sufficient proof of the submarine's existence.

This was not good. He was supposed to meet Juliette at midnight, so all he could do was pray she would show up for that assignation. If nothing else, at least they could bust her and get her back into custody. Still, he hungered to get his hands on DeCristo.

He paced the wharf they'd designated as the rendezvous spot. Lanterns lit the town behind him. A cacophony of music blended. He thought of the night he and Jackie had walked on the beach. He checked his watch. Ten minutes past midnight. He wanted to call the officer who was tailing Juliette, but he didn't want to be on the phone if she showed up late.

Then, his phone rang, the caller ID announcing it was Juliette. Relief slipped over him. Okay. No need to panic yet.

"Hello?" he said, trying to keep the tension from his voice.

"It's not happening tonight," Juliette's voice sounded high and reedy.

His entire body tensed. "When?"

"Tomorrow."

"What time?"

"I'll call and let you know."

Great. More waiting. "I—"

But she'd already hung up. Cursing under his breath,

Scott spun on his heel. He did not like this. It could be a legitimate delay, but it made him uneasy when things did not go according to plan. He stalked to his car, called Carl and told him what was up. Then he called the undercover officer staking out Juliette. "You got your sights on her, Phil?"

"She's at the Hotel Delgado, penthouse suite. I'm in the lobby."

"Are you sure she's there?"

"As sure as I can be."

"Can you get closer than the lobby? I'm scared she could give you the slip."

"I'm sitting right by the elevators. I can't access the penthouse suite."

"Okay," Scott muttered. "Do the best you can."

He went home and tried to get some sleep but insomnia dogged him. Finally, he got up and went to kayak the mangrove channel just as he had the first morning he'd seen Jackie. He paddled past where she had her equipment anchored.

She wasn't there. Thank heavens. Maybe she'd taken his warning seriously. He could only hope so.

The stakeout continued throughout that day. Juliette never called. The fifty thousand dollars of government money that he'd given her burned a hole in his craw. He had a very bad feeling about this.

Finally, he could stand it no more and in the early evening of the third day of the stakeout, he called Juliette and got a message that her cell phone was no longer a working number.

Swearing viciously, he called Phil Drummond. "Has she left the hotel?"

"Not since this thing began," Phil said.

"What about your relief?"

"She said all was quiet."

"Dammit." He pushed a hand through his hair. "Flash your badge at the hotel manager. Get into the penthouse. Call me the minute you find out something."

"Will do."

Scott paced Carl's office. Placed his hands on top of his head. He had a very bad feeling.

Ten minutes later, Phil called back. "Bad news."

"She's gone," Scott guessed.

"Yep."

Scott blew out his breath and reality struck him like a fist to the gut. Juliette had absconded with his fifty thousand dollars and he wasn't any closer to catching DeCristo than he'd been before. He let out a string of curse words. Then he did what he'd been dreading. He called his bosses and told them just how badly he'd screwed up.

"Pull the plug on the whole operation," his boss said curtly. "And when you get back to D.C. there will be a reckoning."

"I might have gotten taken by the woman," Scott said, "but my gut tells me that the small-time dealer Carl arrested is telling the truth about the stealth drone submarine."

"Do you have actual proof?"

"No."

"Then pull the plug."

"If you just give me a few more days… It's time for a shipment. I think that pulling the officers off surveillance of the mangrove channel would be a big mistake."

"Just how much of the taxpayers' money are you willing to waste, Everly? Cut your losses. Bring the officers back in. Now."

13

Under Staffed, Can't Go, that's the U.S. Coast Guard for you. They couldn't find cocaine right under their noses.

—*Drug kingpin Juan DeCristo*

ON THE THIRD DAY AFTER she had spent the night with Scott, Jackie woke up feeling worse than ever. Wasn't it supposed to get better with time? Isn't that the way it worked?

She stayed out of the mangrove channel, not because he commanded her to do so, but because she didn't want to take the risk of running into him.

She tried to concentrate on writing her research paper. Except she was having so much trouble getting fully into the project. This had never happened to her.

Disconcerted, Jackie took a walk on the beach to clear her head, but instead of finding clarity, she'd been painfully reminded of her walks with Scott.

Why couldn't she stop thinking about him? Every time an image of his face popped into her mind—which it did with alarming frequency—her heart gave a strange hitch. Dejected, she tracked back to her apartment, her spirits heavier than ever.

Once inside, she clicked the door closed and sank down onto the couch. Her butt had no more than settled onto the cushion when the alarm went off on her monitor just as it had the evening Scott had messed with her equipment in the mangrove channel.

Adrenaline surged through her veins as all the data recordings disappeared from the screen.

"Here we go again," she muttered, jamming her feet into her sand-dusted flip-flops.

She was in the boat and out on the water before she remembered her promise to Scott that she would not go into the mangrove channel without his go-ahead. Surely that edict didn't pertain to an emergency. She kept driving, headed for the estuary. Besides, he wasn't the boss of her.

Remember how scary it was when you thought he was a drug smuggler?

Yes, but that had been stupidity on her part. If she found someone monkeying with her equipment this time, she would back off and call the Coast Guard. She would not confront anyone as she'd done before. She had learned a thing or two.

It was probably nothing more than the equipment had somehow gotten dislodged. Since she hadn't checked on it since before Megan's wedding; almost anything could have happened.

When she rounded the bend, the sun was starting to slip down the horizon, but it was still an hour or more before sunset. She had plenty of time to at least check things out, if not fix them.

The mangrove channel was completely empty. Not a

soul in sight. The estuary stretched up ahead. No boats. No people. Nothing.

Scott had been alarmist, she assured herself. There was absolutely nothing to worry about.

WHILE JACKIE WAS HEADED down the mangrove channel, Scott sat on the front porch of his bungalow, his cell phone on the small table alongside a half-empty bottle of beer. Over and over again, his mind kept returning to the foiled drug deal. What had he done wrong?

He'd made mistakes, but sitting here doing nothing felt like an even bigger mistake. Yes, his boss had pulled the plug on the operation, but that didn't mean he couldn't continue to investigate on his own. He had to redeem himself for losing the fifty thousand dollars of government money to the conniving Juliette.

He needed more evidence. If only he could talk to the tourist Carl had arrested. Why couldn't he talk to Carl's informant? Maybe he could get something from the guy that Carl hadn't.

Strengthened by having something constructive to do, he got up and headed toward the rental car. It wasn't until he was halfway to the county jail that he realized he'd left his cell phone back on the porch.

JACKIE ANCHORED her boat beside the small buoy she'd put out to mark the spot. Through the wavy blue depths, she could see something big and dark underneath the surface.

What was it?

She hoped the object wasn't too far down. She had brought diving equipment with her, but she knew better than to dive alone. Diving 101. The buddy system or nothing.

But she was just slipping underneath the water a few

feet. She'd be down no longer than she could hold her breath to see what was lurking just underneath the surface.

Probably nothing more than some strange flotsam that had floated up and gotten entangled in the Kevlar cable. Maybe it was simple. She could give it a good shake, dislodge whatever had gotten caught up in her equipment and everything would be right in her world again.

She put on goggles, stripped down to her swimsuit and slipped into the water.

Something had gotten entangled in the cable. But what in the hell was it?

The object was metal. Six feet long. Curious, she cocked her head, ran a hand over the surface. It looked like some kind of undersized submarine. Was it an elaborate remote-control toy?

Her lungs began to hurt. She needed to go topside and get another breath of air. Or better yet, call Scott and ask for help.

Call Scott? No dice. They were through. Calling him now would be like ripping the Band-Aid off a wound before it had a chance to heal.

She turned to head back to the surface, air hunger urgent now, and that's when she spied it.

The thing she'd been searching for.

Her heart took flight and for a brief second she forgot about the need to breathe.

There, darting in and out of the mangrove roots, swam the *Starksia starcki*.

"Why should I talk to you?" the defiant prisoner asked Scott.

"I'll speak to the judge on your behalf. Tell him you

cooperated fully in my investigation. You could get several years shaved off your sentence."

The thirtysomething guy with shoulder-length, greasy brown hair, hangdog mustache and a Margaritaville tattoo on his right forearm looked skeptical. "I've been hearing a lot of reassurances, but I ain't seen any results."

"You haven't come up for trial yet."

"You're not going to catch him, ya know."

"I'll go to my grave trying to put him behind bars," Scott said. "One way or the other, I *will* get him."

The guy slumped in his chair, tossed his head to fling dirty strands of hair from his eyes. "DeCristo never comes to the States. He uses intermediaries. He's too smart to get caught by the Coast Guard."

Scott looked at the folder in his hand. It was one he'd gotten from Carl. "I see you've got a family, Mr. O'Hara."

"Are you threatening me?" The guy hardened his eyes.

"Not at all. I'm assuming you'd like to see them again before you're gray-haired and using a walker."

O'Hara shifted in his chair. "Can you make me any solid promises?"

"I can promise that if you don't help I'll do everything in my power to make sure you serve every second of the sentence you're handed down."

"If DeCristo gets word that I was the one who squealed, he'll kill my family."

"We can protect them," Scott said. "And if you help me, you won't ever have to worry about DeCristo again."

"You underestimate him."

"No, I don't. I fully understand what he's capable of. He killed my father."

That got the guy's attention. "You've got a vendetta against him."

"I do."

The guy thought about it a long moment. "Then maybe you can catch him. It will take someone with a strong sense of revenge to make it happen."

"I'm that someone."

O'Hara said nothing for a long time, then finally he nodded. "Okay." Then he proceeded to tell Scott everything he wanted to hear.

When O'Hara finished, Scott tore out of the jail. He had to get to the mangrove channel *immediately.* According to O'Hara, Juliette had lied about the delivery date. It wasn't two days ago, but now.

The drone submarine was coming up from Cuba this evening.

JACKIE SAT IN HER BOAT, hauling in great gulps of air, feeling both giddy and concerned. At last! She found the Key blenny. Her theory was correct. Her father was wrong.

Was it petty to take joy in being right? Probably. She tried to suppress the smile. Her professor would be ecstatic about her discovery.

But for now she had other fish to fry.

That submarine thing down there belonged to someone and from Scott's warning it was most likely not a friendly someone. She needed to call him and let him know what was going on.

Yes, he was going to lambast her for coming out here, but if she hadn't she wouldn't have discovered the Key blenny.

A fresh thrill of happiness had her shivering in the warm rays of the descending sun. Never mind. She'd put up with the chewing out he was sure to give her because she needed his help dealing with that submarine.

She fished her cell phone from the console on the boat and punched in his number.

It rang several times, and then finally went to voice mail. Dammit. Where was he when she really needed him?

"Scott, this is Jackie. I know you told me not to go to the mangrove channel, but I'm here and I've found the strangest thing—"

The answering system cut her off.

Technology. What a pain. She thought about calling him back and leaving another message, but a sense of urgency told her she needed to get out of here. It would be dark before long and the last thing she needed was to be out here alone if the owner of the submarine showed up to retrieve it.

What to do?

Thoughtfully, she glanced around her boat and her gaze landed on the box that contained her oceanography supplies. She had a tracking device called a D-tag in there that was used to temporarily track whales, dolphins, manatees and the like.

What if she attached the D-tag to the submarine? That way, if it did turn out to be something nefarious, Scott would have a way of tracking the sub.

And if it didn't, you'd lose expensive tracking equipment that belongs to the university.

So what? If it got lost, her father could pay for it. He owed her for not believing in her.

But if she attached it to the submarine, she needed to put on her scuba gear. She couldn't accomplish her task on a single breath of air. It would take several minutes.

Jackie paused, torn.

She knew better than to dive alone. It was the number

one thing drilled into every diver's head. Never, ever dive without a buddy. No exceptions.

But she had no time to go looking for a diving buddy. The sub wasn't that far down. It wouldn't take long to attach the D-tag. One quick dive and she'd be right back. No harm, no foul, no worse for wear.

Okay. Right or wrong, she was making an executive decision, even though she could mentally hear Scott bawling her out.

What he doesn't know won't hurt him.

Taking a deep breath and pushing back the teaching that was screaming "no, no, no!", Jackie got in her diving gear, took the tracking device from the metal box and went over the side of her boat.

She saw the Key blenny again. There were dozens of them, none longer than two inches long. The silver fish with a dark line running down their middles had her grinning wide. They might look insignificant to most people, but Jackie had never seen a prettier fish. She paused a minute to admire her splendid discovery before finally moving on.

The submarine lay about eight feet below the surface wedged in between a snarl of mangrove roots. She swam deeper until she was underneath the sub.

It was inky dark down here. She switched on her flashlight, and holding it tucked underneath one arm, she rolled onto her back to attach the tracking device to the hull.

It took her a good ten minutes to get the D-tag secured. Anxiety at diving alone gripped her. She needed to get out of the water. It would be dark soon, if it wasn't already. Time to head back to Key West and try to call Scott again to let him know what was going on. Besides, she couldn't wait to share her good news with him. He understood what this find meant to her and she realized he was the one she most wanted to tell.

Experiencing an unsettling mix of conflicting emotions—joy over the blenny, smugness at besting her father, guilt over diving alone, hope at the thought of seeing Scott again—she broke the surface and stripped off her mask.

Only to find herself looking at the receiving end of the double barrel of a shotgun.

"JACKIE, JACKIE, JACKIE." Gary Howard shook his head. "Diving alone. I can't believe it. You bad girl."

Jackie sat shivering in her wet suit on Gary's boat, staring incredulously at the man who was her father's assistant. He had the shotgun tucked under his arm and a roll of silver duct tape in his hand.

For one crazy moment, she thought he was here to highjack her research. It was the sort of cutthroat thing he would do. Steal her research, claim it as his own and present it to her father, argue that *he* found the Key blenny. "What are you doing?"

"Isn't it obvious? I'm going to duct tape your hands behind your back."

"But why?"

"You've made a very serious mistake."

"Diving alone?"

"Among other things. But mostly, you found a submarine full of cocaine."

Suddenly everything clicked and she couldn't believe how she'd been so blind. "Y-you're a drug smuggler."

"Who knew? In spite of your measly 138 IQ you are not as dumb as you look."

She kicked at him, but he jumped out of reach, laughing.

"Just for that you get your ankles duct taped together,

too, and before you get any crazy ideas about lunging at me." He set the shotgun down, but simultaneously pulled a small pistol from the waistband of the back of his Bermuda shorts. "I'll just keep this pressed against the back of your skull while I tape up your wrists."

Jackie's heart sank. She was in serious trouble.

Don't give up. Scott will get your voice mail and he will know where to come looking for you.

"I have to thank you for finding the sub. What a stroke of luck," Gary said, "After Juliette flaked on me."

"Juliette?"

"One of the drug mules who was supposed to guide the submarine in with a homing device today, but she's MIA. I pity her. When DeCristo finds out she took off on him, it's not going to be pleasant for her."

"But I don't understand. Why are you doing this? My father pays you a good salary. You have prestige and—"

"You don't get it. Do you have any idea how much money I'm getting from DeCristo? Hundreds of thousands, baby. Not that paltry salary your old man gives me and we both know what a royal pain in the ass he is."

"Who is DeCristo?"

"You are so ignorant."

"Well then, enlighten me."

"DeCristo is an enterprising drug lord out of South America with friends in Cuba. He's found a way to sneak past the Coast Guard."

This was why Scott had warned her not to go into the mangrove channel.

Jackie gulped. She wished she'd listened to him. Yes, she'd found the Key blenny, but she would have eventually found the fish anyway. Now, she was beginning to understand just how foolish she'd been when it was too late to correct her mistake.

Gary duct taped her wrists together, then her feet. Lastly, he stuck a piece of duct tape over her mouth. The jackass. She glowered at him.

He seemed unfazed by the eye-daggers she threw at him. He donned a diving suit. "I'm going to dislodge the submarine and tow it back to the *Anemone*."

So she wasn't the only one stupid enough to dive without a buddy. This alarmed her for her father's sake. If Gary was caught with drugs on the *Sea Anemone,* the Coast Guard could seize the ship. Her father would be devastated. Anger lodged in her throat.

"Be right back," he said.

Jackie fumed. How had she allowed herself to get trapped like this? Regret dug into her. If she hadn't gone off and left her father, he would never have put Gary in charge of the *Sea Anemone* and this would never have happened. She had a lot to make up for.

If you even get a chance.

Surely, Gary wouldn't harm her. He'd known her for ten years. He might be a greedy criminal, but he wasn't a killer.

He's working for a drug lord. There are bound to be henchmen who can do the dirty work for him.

Scott was her only hope of salvation. Maybe he and a team of Coast Guard were staking out the mangrove channel, just waiting to make their move.

Hopefully, she scanned the shore, looking for signs of rescue. Fireflies flickered through the darkness. A mosquito buzzed past her ear. Sultry humidity soaked the air. Her wet suit clung tight and cloying.

She heard nothing more than the natural sounds of the mangrove. Saw nothing that shouldn't have been there. She willed Scott to be there. To find her message and put two and two together, but she knew she couldn't count on it. She had to find a way to save herself.

But how?

Gary came up ten minutes later. He stripped off the wet suit, started the boat and left the estuary for open sea. He didn't speak to her again.

Her hopes plummeted. It would be far more difficult for Scott to track her into the ocean.

You've got a transponder on the sub.

Yes, but Scott didn't know that. He had no way of monitoring the tracking device.

Dammit.

It took almost an hour to reach the spot where Gary had anchored the *Sea Anemone.* She wondered how he was going to explain her, trussed up like a Thanksgiving turkey, to the rest of the crew.

Except when he got to the *Sea Anemone,* she did not know the two men who showed up to greet them. They spoke to Gary in Spanish and helped him pull the submarine up on pulleys beside the ship.

Where were the scientists and students who normally worked on the *Sea Anemone?*

And where was her father? She only had Gary's word that he was at a symposium in Paris. It could all be a lie.

Real fear gripped her then. Her father could be dead. She hadn't spoke to him in months. Not since they'd had their falling-out.

Gary yanked her to her feet, pressed the pistol into her ribs. "I'm going to untie your feet so you can climb onto the ship, but no funny business."

He cut the duct tape around her feet. Briefly, Jackie thought about kicking him, but if Gary didn't shoot her, the two men waiting for them on the deck looked like they would be happy to oblige and put the bullet through her head for him.

Stay alive. You have to find a way to stay alive so you can tell Scott exactly how much you love him.

Yes. Scott. Think of Scott. Even if they kill you at least you will die with the thought of the man you love embedded in your mind.

Love.

Yes. She loved Scott. Loved him with all her heart. Too bad it had taken the threat of losing her life to make her realize it.

Oh, Scott, I am so sorry.

Somehow, Gary pushed her up the ladder and shoved her onto the deck of the *Sea Anemone*. She fell over a tangle of rope. Landed so hard it knocked the breath from her lungs. She lay there staring at the wood floor, smelling fish and thinking of Scott.

Scott. He was everything she never knew she wanted. Patient, but determined. Commanding, yet kind. A solid man who had her back.

Or he would have if she hadn't gotten all jealous and crazy. She'd never gotten jealous and crazy over any man. It had to be love. What else could make a rational scientist act so irrational?

Nothing but love.

She turned the word over in her mind. Felt it in her heart. She loved Scott Everly.

Oh, damn, what a terrible time to know she was stone cold in love. Right when she was on the verge of being killed.

Terrific timing, Birchard.

She would never get credit for finding the Key blenny, but worse than that, without her intervention, the fish could become extinct, forever lost, and that was such a crime. Her heart shredded.

Who was she kidding? The pain came from the thought of losing Scott forever, not the Key blenny. The fish meant a lot to her, yes, but Scott meant a thousand times more.

The two ham-fisted, Spanish-speaking crewmembers hoisted her to her feet and dragged her down the steps to the galley. They threw her unceremoniously onto the couch and then trotted back to the deck.

Minutes later, the men returned carrying white bricks of what Jackie assumed was the cocaine they'd removed from the sub.

Gary trailed behind, his own arms loaded down with the stuff. The three of them made trip after trip, stacking up the galley with it. There had to be hundreds of thousands of dollars worth of product. This was no small-time operation. No way was she getting out of this alive. She knew it now with absolutely certainty.

After they finished stacking cocaine bricks around the room, the two men went on deck while Gary stayed in the galley with her. He didn't speak to Jackie, but instead pulled a satellite cell phone from his pocket and made a call.

From his one-sided conversation she heard him explaining what had happened to the submarine and about finding her in the mangrove channel with it. Was the person on the other end the mysterious DeCristo?

Quick! Think, think. How can you get out of this? You have too much to live for to let this happen. You have to find your father. You have to let Scott know that you love him.

Gary looked pained, glanced at Jackie, then mumbled into the phone. "I don't think that's necessary."

Even from across the room, Jackie could hear a heavily accented voice yell through the phone in English. "I said kill her!"

The man on the other end of the phone had just ordered her execution.

"But she's Jack Birchard's daughter. She's semifamous. She'll be missed." Then Gary went deathly pale. He was trembling so hard Jackie wondered how he was able to keep hold of the phone. "Yes. Yes. I understand."

He hung up the phone and turned to Jackie. "I'm sorry about that."

She wished she didn't have tape over her mouth so she could curse him out.

Gary went to a locker in the back of the room, pulled a key from his pocket and opened up the locker. He whistled and the two men came marching down the steps.

"Load the sub," he told them.

The men reached into the locker, grabbed handfuls of new one hundred dollar bills in fat bundles wrapped in plastic.

Jackie's breath went soft. The pulse at her temple pounded. She'd never been so scared in her life. With the duct tape over her mouth she couldn't even beg Gary for mercy.

Not that I would beg that scumbag for anything. She tossed her head.

"I wish it didn't have to come to this." Gary sighed. "I always did like you."

She threw him a go-to-hell look and notched her chin upward defiantly. Gary didn't have the guts to pull the trigger.

"I've gotten enough of your dirty stares in the past to know exactly what you're thinking," Gary commented. "Yes. I'm too big of an admirer of yours to pull the trigger. Blood does make me a bit squeamish. But Hector and Chemo out there, well, they have no compunctions or aversions."

Jackie gulped. Okay. This was it. She was going to die. Bravely, she met his stare. Bring it on.

"I know, you're tough. I'm truly going to miss you."

Hector and Chemo came back into the gallery and trotted more bundles of money back outside to the submarine.

Gary paced. Sweat popped out on his forehead. The *Sea Anemone* rocked gently on the waves. Well, if she had to die at least she was going to die on the sea. She'd been born on this boat, might as well die on it. Fitting. It was just far too soon.

Funny, she never thought of herself as the marrying kind. Never pictured herself as a mother, but suddenly she realized everything she would miss out on. Love. Marriage. A child. Reuniting with her father. But that was before Scott Everly had come barreling into her life.

Too late. She was too late for all that.

Lost.

She'd lost everything because she'd been too focused and pigheaded. She'd always thought her single-mindedness was her greatest strength. Her intensity. Her ability to fully embrace one thing and embrace it with all her heart.

Now she understood just how unbalanced her life had become. Only lately had equanimity crept in and it was all due to Scott. He'd opened her up. Shown her the joy of just being a regular person. Not Jackie Birchard, daughter of the world's most important living oceanographer. But just Jackie.

Scott. She missed him so much already.

Tears blurred her eyes.

"Ah, hell, Jacks, don't cry," Gary blubbered.

She threw him a look that carried a fiercely obscene message.

Hector and Chemo returned one last time.

"DeCristo said we have to kill her," Gary told them morosely. He handed the gun to Hector. "Take her out on deck. Put her on the edge of the boat so she falls into the ocean when you kill her."

At least she had to give him that. He was giving her the funeral she would have most wanted. Burial at sea. Then he said, "The sharks will take care of her corpse."

Chemo hauled her to her feet. Jackie didn't try to fight or resist. Her mind boiled. As soon as they got her to the edge of the boat, she was jumping in. Yes, unable to swim, with the tape on her mouth, she would drown. But she would rather drown by her own willful act than get shot by these cowardly curs.

The thug manhandled her up the steps to the deck and the second thug followed with Gary's pistol.

Jackie's heart was a snare drum in her ears. Her thoughts were the only thing that kept her calm. Scott. Scott. Scott.

She imagined his arms around her. Holding her nestled in the crook of his elbow, kissing her softly.

Scott.

Tears spilled over her eyes. She was Jackie Birchard. The woman who never cried. But she was crying, not for her life, but for the loss of the man who could have been hers if she hadn't been so stubborn and prideful.

Chemo walked her to the bow. "Get on the edge."

Without protest, she climbed up.

She felt Hector step behind her. *You're not getting a shot at me, buddy.*

She did not hesitate, just stepped off the edge of the ship and into the sea.

As she hit the water, she heard the sound of helicopter blades. A floodlight fell over the ship.

"United States Coast Guard!" came a loud voice over a bullhorn. "Nobody move."

But it was too late. Jackie was already in the water, hands tied, mouth covered with duct tape, dropping down into darkness.

14

I owe my life and that of my daughter to the United States Coast Guard.
                    —*Jack Birchard, renowned oceanographer*

WHILE CARL AND TWO OTHER Coast Guards were in the chopper, Scott and another three Coasties were in the cutter pulling alongside the *Sea Anemone*.

He saw Jackie take a header off the end of the ship just as the sound of a gun going off reverberated through the night.

No! He could not be too late to save her!

Blindly, he dived into the water.

He had to get to her. Had to find her.

Please, God, he prayed. *Don't let her be dead.*

He dived, swimming as hard as he could in the direction of where Jackie had entered the water.

For what seemed like hours, but was only seconds, he kicked through the enveloping ocean. He was too late. Too late.

Jackie!

Then his foot touched something soft and silky.

He reached down. Hair. He grabbed for it. Grabbed

for her. The floodlight from the helicopter brightened the water around him and he could see her below him.

Her eyes were on his.

Mermaid eyes.

She was alive!

He ripped the duct tape from her mouth, tucked her underneath his arms and swam her to the surface.

THE FIRST THING Jackie said to him as they lay on the deck of the *Sea Anemone* breathing in ragged, gulping breaths of sweet air was "What…in…the…hell took you so long?"

Scott grinned. His Jackie. Sassy as always. Laughing, he pulled her to him and peppered her face with kisses.

She hugged him hard.

He hugged her harder.

"I thought I was dead," she confessed.

"Don't ever doubt me, mermaid. I'll always catch you."

Carl came over. "We've got 'em."

Scott looked up to see Gary Howard and two of DeCristo's known confederates standing handcuffed on the deck.

"The cocaine?"

"There's enough cocaine in the galley to send them away for aeons, and there's attempted murder charges to boot, but the submarine is gone." Carl shook his head. "We have nothing to tie the drug delivery to DeCristo."

Scott swore.

"Hey, three birds in the hand is better than nothing, and with this haul you've struck a blow to DeCristo's operation. Besides, now that we know about the stealth drone sub, we can alter our interdiction tactics to counter him. It's enough of a victory for now," Carl said, trying to soothe Scott's mental wound.

"It's something," Scott admitted, but he still couldn't help feeling like he'd lost an important battle.

"Get them out of here," Carl said to the officers holding Gary and DeCristo's two henchmen. The officers herded the drug smugglers onto the Coast Guard cutter that Scott had arrived on.

"You haven't lost him," Jackie whispered.

Scott looked down at the beauty in his arms. The woman he believed he'd lost forever. "What do you mean?"

"I put a D-tag on the hull of the submarine."

Scott frowned. "What does that mean?"

"Oceanographers use D-tags to track whales and dolphins and the like."

Excitement gripped Scott in a tight fist. "You're saying we can track the sub back to DeCristo."

"A sub filled with money. Payment for the cocaine," Jackie elaborated.

Scott's eyes met Carl's.

Carl grinned. "DeCristo is bound to be there to pick up the money. That he's not going to trust to a flunky."

"Jackie Birchard, you are a genius." Scott kissed her hard, hugged her again. "I love you, you beautiful creature!"

"So," Carl said. "How do we go about tracing the money?"

Briefly, Jackie told them how they could track the D-tag she'd affixed to the submarine.

"Chief!" one of Carl's men called out, coming up on deck from the galley. "We've found a man being held hostage in the hold. He's weak and dehydrated but we think it's Jack Birchard."

"DAD?" JACKIE CROUCHED in front of her father.

Carl Dugan's men had brought him out of the hold and eased him down on the galley couch. His lips were dry, his color pale. He looked so frail.

"Jackie," he croaked and reached out to touch her face. "You're here."

She wrapped her arms around him. He was so thin. He hugged her in return. The man was not given to displays of emotion, so the hug shocked her, as did the husky sound of relief in his voice.

"What happened?" she whispered.

In a slow, halting account, he told her how a month earlier he and Gary had argued over Jackie's research on the Key blenny. Her father had decided she was correct and wanted to back her and demote Gary.

Gary had struck him on the back of the head, rendering him unconscious, tied him up and stowed him in the hold. Then he'd dismissed the crew of the *Sea Anemone* and brought on Chemo and Hector.

Guilt chomped at Jackie. While she'd been nursing anger toward her dad, he'd been held prisoner on his own ship.

Scott stood behind her, shifting from foot to foot. She realized he wanted to go after DeCristo and that submarine.

She turned. "What are you still doing here?"

"Supporting you," he said staunchly.

"Scott, there's no need. I'm a big girl. I can take care of my father and myself. Get on that chopper with Carl and go after DeCristo. You need to be in on that interdiction. For the sake of *your* father."

He looked like she'd given him the best present he'd ever received. "You're sure?"

"Go, go. I'll be right here when you get back."

"I won't be long."

"Take all the time you need."

Their eyes met and she felt the full power of his love. "You, Jackie Birchard, are the most awesome woman in the world."

Then Scott was gone, climbing up the steps toward the deck and the waiting chopper.

"You're in love with him," her father observed.

"I am," Jackie said, completely unabashed by her feelings.

She went to the galley kitchen, got him some water and made him a sandwich from what she found in the refrigerator. How many times had she made him sandwiches over the years? It had been their staple meal. Carl had left two of his Coast Guard officers behind to look after her and she made them sandwiches, too.

"Guess what?" She held his glass of water for him as he ravenously tore into the ham sandwich.

He arched an inquisitive eyebrow, his mouth full of sandwich.

"I found *Starksia starcki*."

Her father's eyes rounded in surprise. "You did?"

She grinned. "I did. They were right where I told you they'd be."

"My smart girl," he praised. "You were right and I was wrong."

His praise made everything she'd gone through worth it. "Thanks, Dad."

Then, through a tumult of emotions, they talked, clearing up a lot of old misunderstandings between them. He apologized for not believing her about the Key blenny, and Jack Birchard never apologized for anything. It was the moment of Jackie's greatest triumphant. Garnering not only her father's respect, but his apology, as well.

"I'm not the easiest person in the world to live with, Jackie. I know that and I'm sorry."

"I'm sorry, too, Dad," she said, forgiving him everything. How could she not? He was her father. Besides, she had plenty of flaws of her own.

They talked for hours. She told him about Scott and their evolving relationship. And her father listened. Fully, completely and he wasn't once dismissive.

Jackie stole occasional glances at the clock. She couldn't help fretting about Scott. He was out in deep waters facing off with a drug lord. Anything could happen.

It was one in the morning and her father's eyes were heavy-lidded. He'd been through a lot.

"You need to get some sleep, Dad. We have a lot of stuff to sort out, but tomorrow is soon enough for that. You'll have to go to the police and give a statement about being kidnapped by Gary. It's going to be a media circus."

"We could use the opportunity to talk about the Key blenny." He got up to head for his sleeping compartment. "And how your research is going to save *Starksia starcki* from extinction."

"You mean it?"

"What did I teach you about publicity?"

"When you get media attention, milk it for your own purposes."

"Glad to see you listened to a few things I've said."

"Get some sleep, Dad."

"Your man is going to be all right."

"It's that obvious that I'm worried."

"You love him. How could you not be worried? You have my blessing." Her father smiled. "Not that you need it."

"Thank you. That means a lot."

He leaned over to kiss her cheek. "Good night, daughter. It's good to have you back."

WHILE JACKIE AND HER FATHER were reconciling, Scott, Carl and a cadre of other Coast Guards arrested DeCristo just off the coast of Cuba, retrieving his submarine.

With the help of the device Jackie had affixed to the sub's hull, they'd easily tracked the drone straight to DeCristo. They had more than enough evidence to get a conviction for drug trafficking.

They brought him to Sector Key West where the D.A. was waiting to book the drug lord. The D.A. had even more good news for Scott. They'd found Juliette Sterns through the marked bills she'd been spending and they'd recovered a sizable portion of the money.

Getting through all the red tape took hours. And while Scott was elated to finally have DeCristo in custody, he couldn't stop thinking about Jackie. He couldn't wait to get back to the *Sea Anemone* and share his good news with her.

By the time everything was completed, dawn was pushing up the day with sunny fingers off the Florida Keys. He rushed home, climbed into his boat and took off to where the *Sea Anemone* was anchored just outside the estuary Jackie had been doing her research.

When the *Sea Anemone* came into view, he could see Jackie pacing the bow, clearly as anxious to see him as he was to see her. She wore white shorts and a blue short-sleeved blouse. She caught his eye and smiled broadly.

He killed the engine. "Ahoy there. Permission to board."

"Permission granted. Get your sexy butt up here, Scott Everly."

He dropped anchor and scaled the ladder onto her ship. She flew into his arms and covered his face with kisses. Laughing, Scott kissed her right back.

"How did it go?" she asked.

"We got him. DeCristo is going to spend the rest of his life in jail."

"That's got to be satisfying—avenging your father's death, taking drugs off the streets."

"It is, but you know what's even more satisfying?"

"What?"

"This." He squeezed her tight and kissed her again.

She snuggled against him.

"So how's your dad?"

"He's sleeping. He was pretty exhausted. Gary has been holding him prisoner for more than a month, but he's going to be okay. We had a serious talk about our long-standing issues and ironed out a lot of things."

"That's wonderful."

"He gave us his blessing."

"Oh? What did you tell him about us?"

"That I loved you. I've never said that to a man."

"Jackie," he murmured and buried his face in her hair. "Thank you for saying it to me. I love you with every cell in my body."

Her arms tightened around him.

He glanced over her shoulder. "Where are Carl's men?"

"I sent them home at dawn. There was no reason for them to keep hanging around. Besides, I knew you would be here soon enough."

"That confident of me, were you?"

"Absolutely. Any man who could cut through my emotional wall has to be a keeper."

"So, it's just you and me?"

"You and me and that hammock." She nodded toward a wide white hammock strung between two heavy metal support beams.

"You have a wicked mind, Jackie Birchard."

"It's one of the things you like most about me, admit it."

"Mermaid, when it comes to you, I'm a one hundred percent goner."

She took his hand and led him to the hammock.

MINUTES LATER, they were naked and rocking gently in the hammock, the morning breeze blowing softly over their bare skin. Nothing in her life equaled this sense of celebration as they touched each other, kissed, caressed and sighed together.

She admired his golden-brown skin. His flat belly. His strong muscles. He was hers. This was *her* man. She ran her fingers down to his thighs. He jerked at her touch as if a jolt of electricity had passed straight through him.

"C'mere." He pulled her on top of him, kissed the hollow just beneath her lower lip, speaking against her skin, his words sharp-edged and hungry. "I gotta have you. Right now. No more teasing."

The hammock rocked against their movements.

She splayed her palm over his chest. "Wait."

"What is it?"

"This is it, Scott. A once-in-a-lifetime love. I'm not the easiest person in the world to live with. I can be self-absorbed and cranky and—"

"Strong and brave and honest and tender and vulnerable and tough."

"You make me sound so complex."

"You are."

"Seriously, Scott. Are you sure you're really ready for me?"

"Mermaid," he whispered on a heated breath that warmed the top of her ear, "I was born ready."

Epilogue

When you've found your soul mate, there's nothing to do but plunge into the ocean of love.
—Jackie Birchard, bride-to-be of Coast Guard Lieutenant Commander Scott Everly

SAVE THE DATE EMAIL NOTIFICATION

To our closest friends and family. You are invited to the Fourth of July wedding of Coast Guard Lieutenant Commander Scott Marcus Everly and Jacqueline Michele Birchard at 4:00 p.m. aboard the *Sea Anemone* docked at Wharf 16, Key West, Florida.

We know our union is quick and unexpected, but when you've found your soul mate there's nothing to do but take the plunge. We would love to have the pleasure of your company.

RSVP to Jackie at
JackieBirchard@seaanemone.com.

In lieu of gifts please send a donation to your favorite ecological charity.

Hope to see you in Key West.

* * * * *

PASSION

For a spicier, decidedly hotter read—
this is your destination for romance!

COMING NEXT MONTH
AVAILABLE JANUARY 31, 2012

REQUEST YOUR FREE BOOKS!
2 FREE NOVELS PLUS 2 FREE GIFTS!

Harlequin *Blaze*

red-hot reads!

YES! Please send me 2 FREE Harlequin® Blaze™ novels and my 2 FREE gifts (gifts are worth about $10). After receiving them, if I don't wish to receive any more books, I can return the shipping statement marked "cancel." If I don't cancel, I will receive 6 brand-new novels every month and be billed just $4.49 per book in the U.S. or $4.96 per book in Canada. That's a saving of at least 14% off the cover price. It's quite a bargain. Shipping and handling is just 50¢ per book in the U.S. and 75¢ per book in Canada.* I understand that accepting the 2 free books and gifts places me under no obligation to buy anything. I can always return a shipment and cancel at any time. Even if I never buy another book, the two free books and gifts are mine to keep forever.

151/351 HDN FEQE

Name	(PLEASE PRINT)	
Address		Apt. #
City	State/Prov.	Zip/Postal Code

Signature (if under 18, a parent or guardian must sign)

Mail to the **Reader Service:**
IN U.S.A.: P.O. Box 1867, Buffalo, NY 14240-1867
IN CANADA: P.O. Box 609, Fort Erie, Ontario L2A 5X3

Not valid for current subscribers to Harlequin Blaze books.

Want to try two free books from another line?
Call 1-800-873-8635 or visit www.ReaderService.com.

* Terms and prices subject to change without notice. Prices do not include applicable taxes. Sales tax applicable in N.Y. Canadian residents will be charged applicable taxes. Offer not valid in Quebec. This offer is limited to one order per household. All orders subject to credit approval. Credit or debit balances in a customer's account(s) may be offset by any other outstanding balance owed by or to the customer. Please allow 4 to 6 weeks for delivery. Offer available while quantities last.

Your Privacy—The Reader Service is committed to protecting your privacy. Our Privacy Policy is available online at www.ReaderService.com or upon request from the Reader Service.

We make a portion of our mailing list available to reputable third parties that offer products we believe may interest you. If you prefer that we not exchange your name with third parties, or if you wish to clarify or modify your communication preferences, please visit us at www.ReaderService.com/consumerschoice or write to us at Reader Service Preference Service, P.O. Box 9062, Buffalo, NY 14269. Include your complete name and address.

HBI1B

Louisa Morgan loves being around children.
So when she has the opportunity to tutor bedridden Ellie,
she's determined to bring joy back into the motherless
girl's world. Can she also help Ellie's father open his
heart again? Read on for a sneak peek of

THE COWBOY FATHER

by Linda Ford,
available February 2012 from Love Inspired Historical.

Why had Louisa thought she could do this job? A bubble of self-pity whispered she was totally useless, but Louisa ignored it. She wasn't useless. She could help Ellie if the child allowed it.

Emmet walked her out, waiting until they were out of earshot to speak. "I sense you and Ellie are not getting along."

"Ellie has lost her freedom. On top of that, everything is new. Familiar things are gone. Her only defense is to exert what little independence she has left. I believe she will soon tire of it and find there are more enjoyable ways to pass the time."

He looked doubtful. Louisa feared he would tell her not to return. But after several seconds' consideration, he sighed heavily. "You're right about one thing. She's lost everything. She can hardly be blamed for feeling out of sorts."

"She hasn't lost everything, though." Her words were quiet, coming from a place full of certainty that Emmet was more than enough for this child. "She has you."

"She'll always have me. As long as I live." He clenched his fists. "And I fully intend to raise her in such a way that even if something happened to me, she would never feel like I was gone. I'd be in her thoughts and in her actions every day."

Peace filled Louisa. "Exactly what my father did."

Their gazes connected, forged a single thought about fathers and daughters…how each needed the other. How sweet the relationship was.

Louisa tipped her head away first. "I'll see you tomorrow."

Emmet nodded. "Until tomorrow then."

She climbed behind the wheel of their automobile and turned toward home. She admired Emmet's devotion to his child. It reminded her of the love her own father had lavished on Louisa and her sisters. Louisa smiled as fond memories of her father filled her thoughts. Ellie was a fortunate child to know such love.

Louisa understands what both father and daughter are going through. Will her compassion help them heal—and form a new family? Find out in
THE COWBOY FATHER
by Linda Ford, available February 14, 2012.

Love Inspired Books celebrates 15 years of inspirational romance in 2012! February puts the spotlight on Love Inspired Historical, with each book celebrating family and the special place it has in our hearts. Be sure to pick up all four Love Inspired Historical stories, available February 14, wherever books are sold.